ORPHAN THORNS

FOR ROMAN VISHNIAC'S CHILDREN OF A VANISHED WORLD

Published by JB Stillwater Publishing
Albuquerque, NM

Copyright © 2012 Lynn Strongin. All rights reserved.
Cover illustration, "Rescue" - Copyright © Duncan Regehr. All rights reserved.
Back cover photo: STARSweare, Elana Katz, 2008, Archival Pigment Print, ©2008 elana katz. All Rights Reserved.

No portion of this publication may be reproduced, stored in a retrieval system, or transmitted in any form or by any means, electronic, mechanical, photocopying, recording, or otherwise without the prior written permission of Frances Fanning, unless such copying is expressly permitted by federal copyright law. Address inquiries to Permissions, JB Stillwater Publishing, 12901 Bryce Avenue NE, Albuquerque, NM 87112.

This book is a work of fiction. The characters and scenes depicted herein are fictional. Any resemblance to people, living or dead, or real life incidents, is purely coincidental.

Library of Congress Cataloging-in-Publication Data

Strongin, Lynn.
  Orphan thorns : for Roman Vishniac's Children of a vanished world / Lynn Strongin.
    p. cm.
  ISBN 978-1-937240-06-6 (pbk.)
  I. Vishniac, Roman, 1897-1990. Children of a vanished world. II. Title.
  PS3569.T72O77 2012
  813'.54--dc23
                    2012009676

JB Stillwater Publishing
12901 Bryce Avenue, NE
Albuquerque, NM 87112
http://www.jbstillwater.com
20120313
Printed in the United States of America

TABLE OF CONTENTS:

Prologue 5

PART ONE

Dark under the carousel 1
Botticelli 4
Weight / Wait 5
These Buildings That Die 6
Orphan Lamb 7
This Side of Darkness 9

PART TWO

Adolescence 13
Moravia, Their World 16
Nuclear Rain – A Hail Mary Pass 17
Homer's Rosy-Fingered Dawn 18
The Fashionable Age of Eighty 19
Between the Sheets 20
I Was Born in Breath Knit County 21
Liberty 25
The Body's Betrayal 26
Bach's B Minor Mass 27
I Look Over the Hills 28
Priest 31

PART THREE

The Spelling Bee of Breath-Knit County 37
Mother's Arabian Horses 39
Priests Rise and Fall like husband and wife 40
In Race to stop radiation, a survivor is found 41
By The Falls, where couples marry 42
We Have One very old family photograph 43
The Weight of Treason 44
Sister said for once the weather was beautiful in Berlin 46
If Breath didn't knit this world 47
My Childhood was my comfort 50
Bethany 52
What does a cork tree know 53
Medievally Winter 54

The passer-by of the Downs 57
O Pony 58
Postlude 60
Mother's Arabian Horses 61
Is Algebra from Arabia 62
The Moon in its Pearl & Cradle Skin 64
Have lost my faith 65
In the Previous Life 67
Rolling Wood 71
How Long is the Shelf Life 72
Shall we ever marry? 73
Lamp, Mirror, Door, Wayfarer 75
Slowly healing war's deep wounds 76
the small dish from great Aunt Jane 77
Overshooting the Mark 78
I do not wake, a widow of sand 86
I am the flashlight beside your bed 87
Why is so little taught concerning Icelanders? 89
Sister, when you saw me I had blond hair 90
Iceland 91

PART FOUR

The Translator's Hut 104
The Usual Public Grumble 105
Orphan Stars 106
Rain is the Language of God 107
I am watching stars rise in sky 108
A Bookish Town 110
Half a Pill Slicer 112
Stinks in Here 114

Who is Lynn Strongin **125**

PROLOGUE

Stars we Once Were

Watch out where are returned phoenixes from nests of milk: though children our voice cannot be extinguished our fire the perpetual flame

Not the torch shone under quilts to read by clandestinely as children.

Or later, in hospital (Christ's age when he wandered into the wilderness, that boy)

To pleasure us against coarse linen with numbers like the blue numbers injected under the Jews' skin.

Who can never hear applause, foundlings in a nun's basket left on the revolving wheel for the Mother Superior to find morning come

Unorphaned

By the century that dug the graves.

O for you Love.

    OOO Compassio   Now nurses have entered my life in droves

Like loves, doves homecoming after a battle in Europe has left ground and air smoldering the color of angels wings:

Ash at the burnt tip   rose a heart core:

Down I went like Alice down the hole

Into childhood hospital.

Up I rose like a great big zero   bubble-pipe of clay from yesteryear, yesterday.

PART ONE
STARS WE ONCE WERE

Orphan Thorns

Dark under the carousel

Stars never shine.
A micro-city brought over from Europe
Rodents tunnel deeper runnel thru it
While in the remembered bathroom back home
        Wheat fields out of Van Gogh's delusionary dreams bloom
Blown forever in one direction:
        A cube, it must be a square Kleenex box
Tears of the guests are welcomed.
        One beloved is given one year: a year is a long time.
Imagine a freight train were barrelling at you 100mph down the track
In hat flash second you'd given anything for one more year, hour, fraction of breath
You'd hold it in both hands
Make a flash incision
Put it in your heart to expand the universe.
The concrete Facts of the life in the castle
One favored girlfriend comes every two months: for five hours I plait and unplait her hair
Weaving stories like Rapunzel
Twice a month my husband and I entertain European guests the Alice B Toklas and Gertrude Stun
Of our small harbour own.
Everything in the home has a name
        We fondly speak, or in derision, passing.
O April of all this darkness, you are plighted to keep your troth bring froth flowers uncouth
As a house of the night
As the darkness under the very bright
But chipped deformed carousel horses.
Holding our courses
We lament, we despair, and youth lungs keep clapping thin moth like

Lynn Strongin

hands on the air. The all-but-deserted air.
Mark Twain and Abe Lincoln
Reading them in bed at age seventy-two
I remember being fourteen.
The jury's still out.
Earth was a micro life: amusements parks in lurid summer
Ice palaces in winter
Yet I straddled that black ball
The darkness doesn't bypass me: nothing does at all:
Detritus, exquisitely preserved old photographs in star balls, glass over roll by under the carousel.
What is the horse's whirling to their whirling?
What am I doing so early on a pill for pain?
I can write people "You're a gem: one in a million," and the message will be hold your tongue I do not want to be bothered by emotion.
We are all sick from not wanting to be bothered by emotion.
Bother me, darling
Here is a raggy string bear from the end of time:
Some child must have dropped him hr the slats in the merry go round floor: who is to say he is
Or isn't (like you) mine?

Orphan Thorns

Under the boardwalk
Like at the blue movies, a nickel Fridays,
It was different: velvety like midnight, but slats let in shafts of air, you could look up at sky.
Heaven was projectile, blasting down thru those peepholes like gusts of prairie air stirred to a cyclone in canvas but one wore no red shiny pumps down under.
The one time the call for help came like coiled wire over the miles
I was imagining myself as two kinds of canine:
The old RCA Viktor dog, ears cocked back barking beside black trumpet
Then the delicate greyhound lean outracing the bus
Lapping up the miles. It was a dog's life.
I stood stock-still
I heard the Lord coming over the furthest hill
Evoking a kind of nostalgic in a fairy tale.
Before a wine began to blow above the keyboard
Fire burned: early summer sun.
Mother promised me I would learn all twenty-four letters by the time summer was done.
Rather I learned to endure the burning of scalding wool
Holding still as mummy, child of twelve, worth mouthing first poems:
Thought I could learn no more of isolation when the Broken Man came.
But
Books propped at either side
My flanks sheltered by literature
The dialogue that wakes in the heart of darkness
The heart that beats out the pain like a jungle drum.

BOTTICELLI

Just the summer you reached the age of Botticelli's "Primavera,"
You developed a curvature
Of the spine.

Leaves shook down
Florentine. The decision was taken
Not to return.

Your mother found you Yoga
Practitioner
(You had the long limbs, flower-stem neck of a dancer.)

A bodice lifted your small high breasts
You were one summer under Juliette's
Age.

It was a tense autumn: stretched
To breaking--
Yet in this time of my life, I feel so high--I forget to breathe at times.

Do I flash? -- Not with the adolescent sheen of leaves
At the top of olive trees:
I speak with those who drive to the apple orchard in this storm:

If I gleam, it is that I am
Gnarled roots, a street fighter--all Tuscan.

WEIGHT / WAIT

You drove out to the apple orchard in storm.
I lay low--pricing a titanium wheel
chair to replace this slow one.

After having a crown put back in my mouth
where I knocked teeth in a fall on my face as a child
of twelve--old post, tricky operation.

I fell half a century. The world was just patching itself up after war.
You drove home
with windfall apples.
  *
Tree bore the weight of fruit:
floor bore the weight of my body
the marble caught my weight.
  *
Last night
I was frightened
as though I might be captured, then shot at dawn.

But dawn broke clean. My Roman Catholic sister in the South has had her operation;
Now I've put my reindeer boots on--
to wait for the telephone to ring; and light a vigil candle for my nun.

Lynn Strongin

THESE BUILDINGS THAT DIE

                                        at the edge of sleep
are the ones that become transparent
every evening while I wait.

I watch film of our family touring Dubrovnik
so young--legs long,
someone spooning yogurt out of Dannon, crossing a square in Prague.

The Slavic soul: before the nine-hour cancer operation,
an Adonis, before historic stone.

ORPHAN LAMB

For your work, you travelled to another country
my country
having renewed your passport.

    When you flew back home to this island, now our home,
    a fogbound airport
    made you turn around.

    So you bought Rand McNally
    roadmaps and
    took the ferry home.

    *

What was it like to stack over our island,
above the small airport
on half an hour's fuel, just floating?
    *
For this work,
you had exchanged this currency
for the big land's;

All one-color green. Dull as ditchwater, low on exchange.
The clocks turned back next day--fatigue was water rising.
Your travel alarm went off from your valise the first meal back home.
    *
By the time,
the red corduroy winter jacket arrives,
It will be too late. The night you came home, I knew autumn had done.

Winter has come.
I wear an old jacket.
Leaves appear to have lost body, turning to pure light:

I remember the high desert:
sleeves of rain:
Mexican grates with iron leaves, roses of iron

But mesquite light
no weight--pure floating,
pinion burning:

Lynn Strongin

    Our Southland, thin, heady oxygen: our
driving up to Taos, taking a wrong turn on a dirt road,
finding in the crystal cold, the Pueblo family feeding (with baby bottle and
nipple)
                      an orphan lamb.
(October 26, 1998)

This Side of Darkness

You danced this side of darkness--
but darkness came down
in a sleeve, like a cone spinning

tornado
a cocoon,
ballerina of thirteen.

> You kicked the cloud--cool,
> with your
> amazing extension.

But every shadow of dark blue
named
and unnamed opens.

> You
> sighed,
> "It runs in the family."
>   *

Mother ran it down--like a hound on the hunt:
(guilt in the blood)
while you danced on--fabulous, unrelenting.
(Oct, 1998)

PART TWO:
HOMER'S ROSY-FINGERED DAWN

Adolescence

                broke--a subdued storm:
I see you in a milky darkness
like ink.

Dancing.
At ten, you loved cups with ears, and
the home blooming with the smell of ironing

even those nicotine
roses
in asbestos charmed you.
            *
In Holland
with a sky flat as a sermon--there were brick step-roofs and bell-roofs
blazing

you drew chimneypots, windmills you danced
you visited Anne Franks' home
--you later were to dance her at thirteen.

       *
You became a Kirov kid
at twelve,
the age when I became one of the block of ward-children.

But I heard the music of the spheres
then--all
lined up.
      *
Barely into your teens,
you develop a curvature of the spine
which my nun friend says is the reason you blazed so brightly.
             *
There's a specialist in Iowa
and one
in Durham.

There's
a brace,

Lynn Strongin

and there's an operation.

Your mother asks herself
if the soul can peel from the body
like bark from a willow.

Dipping my pen,
I ask
can dance take the place of happiness?

II.
Saint Augustine
believed we live two lives:
one in the daily world, one in the divine.

Does your foot still rise and fall
in the Wheatfield of the studio in morning?
the floorboards catch the winter shine?

Like light in Monet's garden:
off-white the ballet slipper,
milk-stone.
*
Down to basics:
math tutoring, a tall
glass of water in Southwest morning.

That geometric curve Euclid drew--
makes me think of the royal necks of swans.
I see triangles this morning, winter wind

lifts the breast feathers of the wren.
The geometry of our loss:
Those windows that die along my horizon each evening

at the intersection where I wait
under a clear moon
dissolve.
*
Second to breathing--dancing.
I see you at the ballet in milk darkness
only last winter

on the brink,
a Degas--but more careful, drawn in whitish ink
just before first snowfall, before adolescence broke like a whip cracking
just before you turned thirteen.

Lynn Strongin

MORAVIA, THEIR WORLD

The Mandau.
Moon-lightning.
Dawn coming up white as an onion.

Nailed to a choice,
trapped by ageing strength--
you appeared to me, startling

as a solarized photograph
of salt marsh hay
lit by lightning, particular, in a treacherously brightened day.

Nuclear Rain – A Hail Mary Pass

I am sending you this lot to bring you to your knees:
Locked the door (these four walls) thrown away the keys.
It doesn't matter how many you say, Hail Marys.
I wanted a Hail Mary Pass, like a gym pass
And a little silver whistle such as the gym coach wears
Never to be seen with naked eye or lens
Inside the yard of Oxen bridge Prison again
Or Saint James Infirmary
 but...

Radioactive rain fell upon the child who had lived, dreamed, spoke at a white colonial home built blue shutters close to the sidewalk: the home had the comfort look of a watercolor by a gifted amateur This was our child who kept sewing herself in black sacks double over knees toes at chin, this is the child of ours who flattened herself against sheets, white lump turned back into the womb

And who colored herself out

Colored her white. Diamond baby, Baby diamond. Bibb lettuce your color eye.

But the country is now facing a cascade of accumulating problems that suggest that radioactive releases of steam from the crippled plants could go on for weeks or even months.

The electric pump grid went down

How cool the fuel?

Nerve of light, I am thinking about such nerves: she was all nerves the child

No Hail Mary Pass can get her out of this now.

HOMER'S ROSY-FINGERED DAWN

"Armed with the power of Thy Name nothing can ever hurt me, and with Thy love in my heart the world's afflictions can in no wise alarm."
                    Thai meditation

Who engineered the rosy-fingered dawn?
Fiery
yet lyric.
          *
Who engineered the world's afflictions?
Can you bring your next-of-kin to court?
If you get detained in a court case this winter--what then?

Where will the protecting wings
be?
Will you believe still in love's wellsprings?

"The Velvet Revolution"
they called it
at first.

The Czech Republic and Slovakia the states became.
After, they called it, irreparably, in lowered tones:
Loss   and separation.
(Oct 26, 1998)

THE FASHIONABLE AGE OF EIGHTY

The small ones are the mighty ones.
Mother has
reached the fashionable age of eighty.

I see every shade of brown for her room;
Holland cloth,
dark, beet-red roses.

Maybe,
I am getting old
myself

Everything these days haunts me:
A lawn of a thousand frost flakes;
a thousand-flower winter sky of stars.

Which side of darkness do I stand on?
Foxy --this waking:
You cannot land in fog--so fly home a second time.

You did not cry at fourteen
You fell from a horse
and were stitched blind.

Like the soldier
who rarely spoke
of his Prisoner of War time.

Speak to me,
let it blossom now
or your strife will seed home and bloom in some darkly bright thing
thorn flower in spring.

Lynn Strongin

BETWEEN THE SHEETS

I wanted to be between the sheets with you.
Instead a ploughman's lunch:
Atonement, attrition, Black Sunday.
and from "Her Majesty's Stationary Office"
The authorized child-care book.
A bear with button eyes.
Felt pads of feet, such soles.
A ribbon at the neck. Blow or mauve? Wanted to sit on his nose.
Not a dream baby, a magical baby, a duplicate in implicate order.
Amsterdam. Atonement. Wanted all these, a toss of stone in the hand.
Instead I got straws, bent ones, slow drawing.
Tossed them in the sand for the sand to drink thru them.
What would come up? Would it be a water cool and limpid
Like our first kiss?
      I wanted to be between the sheets with you: carved in stone,
written in water in liquid black ink script. You'd never allow anyone
calling me crip
Only with your eyes, never your lips. Not the last game we played. Not
this.

I Was Born in Breath Knit County

Beside a small inland sea
In lace county.
Not thru the lane called Irish lace
I could grow my hair long and braid it.
But it always was too fine.
"You have no idea how much I care for you!" said the Greek woman.
It seems the leaves never fell this autumn:
They just stayed, actors poised for their entry
Then it was curtains
Where was winter
Where the certain
Love-lock that throws away the key?
If they touch this blue kid, she'll zoom right on up out of the bed.
"Sprite!" she rose and put one hand on either cheek.
I have known one or two women who have slid off their wedding ring in the course of our conversation and said "I don't know whether or not to wear this."
At times I lived on margins, at others in the core of the terrifying cycles of life.' In my lover's eyes I saw unending wheels spinning
Catherine wheels
Pinwheels. My translator, coiled, curled dark child
Turning into wild bird
Unlike my love who folds gracefully
It's terrifying, brilliant the stork. Don't interrupt me please

We must move on in our strange unease
The bowl licked clean by the cat
The pony
Whippt for reprimand
The love who came back for more despite
A thunderously killing week: shoulders bent, whipped
Hair blown back
Accept clipped
and hairdo memorized down to the last sray spitcurls to forehead
strangely right
despite the poet's Yankee accent
combined with Southern drawl
The Saxon language was never, like a dollhouse, my home:
The rooms were strangely off angel

The padding soles of the feet late at night when one rises for a taste of us all: lace tea-stained, stained, ecru paper
Tattersall beret your uncle William, a Victoria child with a touch of the exotic Jew from Roma after all
He tatty beret hung at a perfectly rakish angle as though poised for a portrait
Casual
Disaster strikes the head of the family, the boy born to be a curl
Edwardian lace necklace which looks as f it might fly away from us all

The bucket of tears cried For Lesbia, for Willy the cat, Moon globe her mother and flood, the little blood-
Colored half breed whose whiskers make him look like a dog in an Italian pantomime.
His stance beat the pants off the mathematician's get-up:
Harlequin in his satins tries to entertain you, translator, magician:
Despite being the almond flour for Jewish Passover ground in a Southern mill:
marbles in a glass mustard jar are small planets having stopped their spin:
Orphaned, but starred well: down to every last sing dot on paper:
Hang on it your wind-breaker darling boy-girl
And let rest for a night or a thousand white nights of Pushkin or Tolstoy
A thousand bleak dreams of Dostoevsky:
List-maker you culled the making of his world:
Jacket khaki on the one bent, slightly burnt topsoil color
Of its hook, its latchet, call it what you will : its nail:
The weather over the hill will be what it will
Painted in frame by morning till fog blows it off
To the second weather of the wheys of the mill, this churning world.
I'm a blade runner in my rainbow wools
Driven each of four directions of this world
Loser of that war:
    A stack of paperback mysteries throws its shadow like the man with tip hat
The bent man coming

Not far off now
    Cartographer, who drew battle's strategy maps with a passion and Paschendale's pen: will he, will she make that last climb until
All the valley is laid like silver for the last supper: still

As the most unruffled pond in a panting the table holds each object
All the colors robbed from the till.
Sure as the Lord made little green apples,
Yours till the cows come home, ill hell freezes over
(though you won't get to reading this poem).
Stamina is our name, sister Sloan.
Keep us close, Press us, bloxon, dark voiced, translator, librarian, poet:
Mother of us all, I give you my heart which I cut out of my body
Starred   like the sky:
Like the asylum orphaned.
   The latter evenings of my childhood were riddled by cod liver oil mixed with milk of magnesia radium-white,
   Unforgiving: why should it e forgiving? What was the punishment? What the crime?
   The later letters of my evening are
        holding you in safe-keeping.
   Energizers.
   They cause the voices which haunt you, 'You're only a switchboard operator, you're a keypunch girl,"
   The words of father and mother come with a curl
   Like the curvatures in a spine of iron.
   You pin your long hair up: tonight you take it out upon yourself by a long evening of steam ironing:
   The clouds will pillow, roll, throw some fast punches, a left hook, a right hook,
   A filthy look such as drives you thru the floor of hell
   Where you have been thrashed like wheat till so blond-thin you resembled a leukemic kitten:
   You cried till the back of your eyes were dry. The lord of the bed sheets had had a good talking down, a tongue-lashing: you lashed yourself to your infamous parents' infamous last words: this was lie shafting thru the four chambered organ with a steel needle the innocent heart of baby birds:
   Carbon copy God on this one.

At cock crow in Breath Knit Lane, the weathervane will radiate black iron

The voices may stop at last: mother and father bantering

Or at the brown dusk

You will be happy again. "If I end up in an institution who will shave me? I don't want to look like a female Abraham Lincoln" you think.

You think depressed people do not make good company. You think of buying boxes of diapers for a bladder infection in your seventies.

I think of your opening Dante late at night, sipping wine, smiles. I think of my years at the music academy.

My Thursdays were riding an elevator up floor after floor, the trumpet came thru the elevator on the first floor, the violins, the voice ascending at the top.

Harmony first thru fifth species counterpoint Miss Ulelha

Who wore the neck scarves of the 1950's tightly tied at the neck as if to strange,

Carried her handbag by the handle in front of her as women did in those days over half a century ago: like a handlebar.

Would I sit in a brown coffeeshop with you I would be enjoying myself, listening in the moment

But listening more sharply for when Sweet Pea came, the long note of the trumpet

Winding up, down spiral stairways, belief in the self, the power of the voice growing, growing till wings burst thru shell of sound, feathers shone

But my lover does not want to hear the German-Jewish voice of my past in an interview

The cock crowing.

Liberty

I did not make the trip.
I did not wear out shoe-leather,
I did not make the aborted landing, going to one land from another, in winter's raw ether.
*
I was the one waiting
face like
Roman stone.
*
It was the winter of our faith.
No traveler's
advisory came.

If I am the safe harbor,
the abiding presence, then
understand:

it is not easy listening to the weather
rarely voyaging:
it is not easy standing like the Statue of Liberty

head wreathed in fog,
but blind, feet frozen at the gate of the great-lost city I call home.
Orphaned children, orphan stars we once were who now lie in a ward
transferred to an operating theatre
where God
s light does down upon us shine:
the nurse's purple bag crushed softly, chamois-like, in the corner like bruise but beatifically bruised purple plum.
(Oct 1998)

Lynn Strongin

The Body's Betrayal

Defeated by the circumstance?
you go out--glance at birds pale as shell.

By now, breath stains air. The spell. (Was it a boy, or a girl?)
You feel as though an apple tree fell on you.

But morning in the studio
puts a fresh face on things;

brush strokes strip old wood
of varnish and paint.
*
It was no avalanche
but the girl who leapt quicksilver this side of night,

What if pantomime
could replace dance? What if dark were exchanged for light?
*
What does God want?
A substitute? A transference?

The reward of a hundred martyrs
and service in both worlds?

Birds pale as shell.
The body, at thirteen, its exchange, its betrayal.
(October 1998)

Bach's B Minor Mass

I go out and buy Bach's B Minor mass
the one he wrote for no known reason

except love for God.(O Kyrie, My Ellison.)
Glacial, North inches in.

Or if there was a reason--
it is not clear

to man.
Kept company these nights by the Mass,

expecting no urgency
other

than being profoundly alone
I watch a few late birds, colder than

ever stain
like breath the dark air : like feathered stone.

I Look Over the Hills

The pearl skin of the moon is a milk skin.
Here is the cape, there the footsole.

Radon Rabbit, I open the book and think of Icelandic reindeer
Rainbow runners, knit Irish wool on feet
And the back
Always the weight of rocks and fox in the back
Payload pain.
Men in moonwalk suits
Pearl skinned women dive for keepers.
Bonneted in the skullcap, laced, of the newborn.
This may be a supermoon
But did it bring quake and tsunami on?
In our Amish bones,
In our Mennonite discipline and Hebrew tradition
in our Quaker hands and shoes
Did it run the rainbow thru us like radiation? Did we chose a love beyond which
There can be no bruise no bruise.

Carrying me home music manuscript pages thru the night
While dark knits stars into place, home
To receive black ink, mother has made another trip to Pedelson's Music supply store, amply stocked in New York City.
As the white goat receives black hail
Raw toothed girl, I stash the catch, hug it to me like mail.
The excitement of words kicking in the womb like the child
Wearing embroidered wools, tousled dark blond hair cut like a pudding bowl, I wrestled (heart in my mouth) with my demons and angels.
In the barracks, nights rolled thin as parchment cigarette papers, our famous, infamous coffin-nail lighting Sobranies Black Russians.
Tonight is a cosmic event: a supermoon
One takes the sons hunting by turns: for books, for vocations, for girls.
Is it possible to raise good men?
Shoes chafe, fingers cramp, one doesn't say a word, big toes swell up at the ends
Giving them the shape of small hammers.
Remember: there are volcanologists.

A sample of tap water from Tokyo shows a tiny level of radioactivity.
The last option would be entombing the plant with concrete and sand to
prevent a catastrophic radiation leak, the method used at Chernobyl in
Ukraine in 1986
Think of me when you go to speak with the angels above Byzantine
temples,
Think of me, take the lens for legs (Star-rod-city sways on poles): Wake up,
owls.
When you navigate with minutely detailed maps
England's and Holland's canals.

The marriage had begun to unraval
Said the woman who under her breath said Hail Marys: the small brick
townhouse had a gravel driveway definitive as the judge's gavel.
She kicked the firedogs, dark bronze.
And over the counter by day spread linen tableware, napkins that fit
perfect silver rings.
Desperately at the bottom of a ditch coaxing out sun on a dark day.
It's a sign of the love that she cleaned up pools after me
When I felt shames to leave circles of sat urine like a fourteen year old boy.
Where can we go, how be to be as we used to be?
The tap water, spinach, milk radiated above government safety levels.
The boy jumps a fence to beat the alfalfa to raise a hare
But no Coney is there.
Does she know how it knifes me thru the gut, lifts me by the hair
Not to be able to take the car any more out of here?
She knows. I dare
Say that's the cause of her anger.

If only Anne could kill the voices like kittens in water.
doused
One by one shoebox by shoe, her mother's raspy soliloquy's, her father's
gin-fueled omens.
Every time I meet her, there's a catch light in her eye.
Is the rasp and latch the door doing its final close on those monstrous
fellows?
Care for a drop? I hold forth licorice.
She'd rather Jim Beam. Or Brandy. No eye candy.
She polishes off a drink of Red Bull. Nearly all.
In rainbow runners, unlike snowshoes, or skies she blades into the
darkness of her wonder, the thunder so loud of her unease.
Her country, her people are elsewhere everywhere shaking drums of fear

Lynn Strongin

Leather dusk as meadows under snow
Yonder: will bone needles like pine needles ever work for her like litanies?
Card catalogues? Bee breviaries?
What if, in heaven, there is to be at last a great reprise?

Priest

(ANOTHER TENSILE DAY)

"the magic that glows along a threshold, around a certain biscuit tin" (David Malouf)

Stretched to breaking point,
the orchard:
fruit is difficult to keep

in early cold. Austerity
till
Chopin plays, saying--sheer heart is allowed.

The music whispers, soft at first:
then full, out out.

Lynn Strongin

I go out in black and white--
Like a priest
Touching the red hem of winter day.

What glows is under the lintel, around the tin. Wind wrests the breath from me.
It comes from the
Northeast.

The hospitals, I knew in my youth,
The schools I pass
Is half a century?

Back at least.
My link with sick children
Harrowing, natural is the last

Lit fuse (it glows under the threshold, around the biscuit tin) it glows
Along the sky:
I know these griefs by heart--like his beads, the beadsman.
(October 27 1998)

Orphan Thorns

O Carrissima!
Exclaimed Jane, the nurse clasping her hands
Wonderful, widely traveled hands that have turned the body of a person in pain
That has navigated the rivers of my heart
The inland waterways
And the cold clear sealed Artesian well of childhood.
O Artemis. O Arterial access, Amen to Aphrodite. Women have it all, breathing out and in two wings like silk butterflies.

With spikenard and incense
We spike the pain by unkind words, not flat-out mean but flung
Slung.
They land by the four-poster Quaker bed we sleep in.
Life in the beginning was all dash and daring, slamming around the pad in moth eaten sweaters with holes at the elbow.
I think of her, the nurse, up before dawn, down late, late:
I turn a page of winter, winter that is my fate. No ornamental beauty
In the lovely deep snow, who knows how many meals I have to go before sleep?
The incline toward dying is steep
The raw, glassy like objects of life may break.
Love is more than mere sleep to the atrocities of the world: I know sparrow
Who knows the marrow.
But to the bone
Dug the post on which the flag of my spirit is flung. Stars we once were who will ever be
Once shinning down from the heavens
Now shining up from the grave
Opened: orphan voices of children fly out, the sharpest notes thorns: the blood on the side Chinese red lacquer
The ruby or the mown down, renowned, rising phoenix from the fire. Beware. Here comes ignition. I cannot take the fear away says to the nurse but we are never alone.

PART THREE
O CARISSIMA!

THE SPELLING BEE OF BREATH-KNIT COUNTY
(FOR HUGH FOX, TOUJOURS)

A small boy named Leopold
Came down one morning from his bed chamber
And wept biter
So that the bright ears ran over his cheeks.
                School Reader, Second Book, 1849 New York
                published by Dayton and Saxon.

Penelope,
Pertelope, come to me:
I will tell ye spelling bees of Breath-Knit County

At cock crow in Breath Knit Lane, the weathervane will radiate, black iron

The voices may stop at last: mother and father bantering

Or at the brown dusk

You will be happy again. "If I end up in an institution that will shave me? I don't want to look like a female Abraham Lincoln" you think.

You think depressed people do not make good company. You think of buying boxes of diapers for a bladder infection in your seventies.

I think of your opening Dante late at night, sipping wine, and smiles. I think of my years at the music academy.

My Thursdays were riding an elevator up floor after floor, the trumpet came thru the elevator on the first floor, the violins, the voice ascending at the top.

Harmony and first thru fifth species counterpoint Miss Ulelha

Who wore the neck scarves of the 1950's tightly tied at the neck as if to strange,

Carried her handbag by the handle in front of her as women did in those days over half a century ago: like a handlebar.

Would I sit in a brown confessor coffee shop with you I would be enjoying myself, listening in the moment

But listening more sharply for when Sweet Pea came, the long note of the trumpet

Winding up, down spiral stairways, belief in the self, the power of the voice growing, growing till wings burst thru shell of sound, feathers shone

But my lover does not want to hear the German-Jewish voice of my past in an interview

The cock crowing.

Mother's Arabian Horses

                    Ripple on silk batik   catch up with their tails:
Breathless. Out of heart but rich dark hood:
In the name of blood,
    I spent morning reconstructing a ruined pillow, delicate as hand surgery, ball by ball of cotton
    Trolling on from a narrow escape
    My finger shedding a fragile light
    Like veil.
    An Arabian batik stork flashes temperamentally his silk tail.
    Cottonwood dust flickers over barbecues coals, bats will soon take blue-black wing.
    This is nothing to the killing season
    When we came.
        Living on Cook Street, down from Wellburns Grocery Family Owned and Operated for over a century (And what a century in which all those soldiers live dand died, wallpaper backdrop gunmetal gray) up from the Ocean and Oxford Foods.
    Fort Street, "Antique Row" obliquely laddering up and down
        our salvation.
    I wanted to do anything to turn back, crying O native land where the brightness was culled in a basket like bird feathers
    Of the mounting swan
    Not the shot swan.

Lynn Strongin

Priests Rise and Fall like Husband and Wife

I want to get over it all:
Over and under   O pall
Crows wings shoeblack blackening everything.
I don' want to look at the basket of *her* mail, this is my homecoming.
My oak trails in the twilight haze of a hundred Canadas.
This is the one I have come to:
With girl, grown pale from being a domestic. Six weeks' time
A long spool and a short one.
Break Knit county films over like chainmail behind glass.
I have decided to spring for "The Stuff or Dreams are made of"
Because that is the fire colored wool I card in my hands
To play cat's cradle
Each bleached objects, wood, glass marbles
   The hog head butchered, hung in the shop window suggesting ruby, impaled archangel
   To weave a scarlet cloak for the infant king.

IN RACE TO STOP RADIATION, A SURVIVOR IS FOUND

Coal-haired, no blonde: her arms waving like a wand.
That is you, sister, hands trust deep in long raincoat pocket, trench coat belt drawn:
Or history in the clod of blood breathes against Berlin nightfall. So much for Amsterdam. So much for Atonement.
Nippon's unprecedented multiple crisis of earthquake, tsunami and radiation leak.
Reminds me of Father coming in clip chart in hand
With the manna, the verdict.
Gazing out a Manhattan window over Oriental slanting rain. WE are the innocents, we are the attacked
The cliff dwellers and the ghetto haunters (I see you in a new light, a new weight)
In atticks, in cellars
In all that was left you and me
After much was taken away:
Brick-by-brick
Pearl knit-by-knit. My head cracked like ice-cubes when I was in great pain.
Sweater returns, one arm missing
To Breath knit Count.
    Secure, going to the Legislature for lunch, reservations in hand
The old couple, he with a fedora and feather-in-its brim, spats, watch chain on fob
She fit to kill: old lady shoes with flat black heels but listen, lambkin, her hose with violet roses.
Red shoes no knickers. We smiled, like Auntie Glo, the G bird boarding with her pass the A train
Amtrak: forever survivor, forever beating back radiation, Beanie cape of younger angel, brown, firm as soil in spring, planted on.

By The Falls, Where Couples Marry

Between two countries
A postcard romance takes place, wt and wisdom loss and longing:
The forked creatures bows, takes vows
I dare see Auntie Glo radiating from Kingman and Barstow to up our island.
Before frolicsome falls.
Our baptismal font
Is below the joists of golden wood stashing love letters cadging away for a rainy day
Oyster Creek, speak to me, speak
My son the swan stood tall: my aunt, at eighty, in wheelchair leg bags flapping like wings
With the keepsake, powder-blue feather duster from her Portuguese homemaker of fifty years, she closes her eyes: she sees Japan, she hums, open the album:
Stirring memories of Japan's nuclear history
The shattered glass
The shattered bones
The rape of radiation.
No morning can be radiant when this is gong on.
Anne, remember you are not just the one who plunges us in darkness
Pulls the plug on light.

We Have One Very Old Family Photograph

    which held up to the light is pure shine: then pressed to the walnut coffee table with a photographer's glass loop:
    made in a shaft, children handcuffed dare the devil.
    Unwell, much closed to them
    They know the veins, which are richest, are emptied:
    The gold that pours out of them
    Pure heaven,
    Poor hell. Energizes us
    Like a horseshoe rod the horseshoe.
    Secrets you tell your doll get darker and darker in the freeze:
    Till she's on knees
    Her wooden lips freeze. (When will you cash your one thousand loto slips in? even check on them
    Grindstone, soapstone, clearing out for the mill.)
    Please God let you make the trip to come met me, soldier boots covered with flowers
    I have become better since I tried for the prize.
    Miners and canaries: glassine envelopes
    Here is my heart-pounding adventure packet.
    I have so long yearned to see you: fields of steel behind glass
    Surrounded by Queen Anne's lace
    In the Holland etching, love in a little lithograph.

The Weight of Treason

Is thin, watery, casts shadow like water in glass jar:
I know where you are, the true vanilla.
Won't pass.
　　The story that flows past my window like water
Carrying paper darts, wet maps: Brazil is bent, knees buckled then there are
　　Rucked up skirts of Panama:
The bushes are pulled backwards, girls their hair backblown
and the child's hands are sticky from the small boys of *Crayola*.
Pain goes to my head like bubbles in a glass of champagne: they do not come to a standstill.
Mulberry-colored fork of haymaker rising in gray fields, a face glistens thru branches onto the roofs of Breath Knit, the smallest town in the township. What is a town ship?
A ship that goes nowhere. Longing to get out of the pain is an endless knot, representing the intertwining widow with compassion. It's also the symbol of infinity, unity. I am united with my past; it grabs me by the heels hurls me round like a newborn.
　　I feel like a haymaker resting in fields
Rocks, beehive hairdos of the fifties, cones of gold hay rising behind me finishing the equation.
　　This life.
　　Where radiation workers are made to sleep amid pools of cooling field rod desperate to keep them cool
　　Lying down in white, austere as the Austens:
Some of us are soon to pass form this world: wearing white, moon suits,
　　Plutonium leaking into soil and water. To wake up to rad rods, where does one take one's life from here?
　　Once inhaled is there forever, thousands of years.
　　And we have cavil at home.
　　What is its weight? The heavy, grape-dark, oppressive weight of treason.
　　Tell me, conductor of choruses: where do I take my life from here?

We are knit by-Breath and Weather, brother and sister, darker, brighter: for worse, for better, elbowing pipeline under the city: the verification of life by inspiration: red mufflers against sore throats, but they are always sore when speaking the truth, letter by letter.

Blue horses blaze night alleys

Even in a lit match, they would have yellow teeth:

Even in a knockdown drag out the winner, whoever one would be a thief.

A nest hangs from a belt of leather

Will it draw featherings ?

Get real draw together.

Like slipping out of a date, a colony

Sliding over gunshot romances

A lithely oiled tether

The true vanilla.

Lynn Strongin

Sister said for once the weather was beautiful in Berlin

A freak.
An old couple here, going for lunch at the legislature chat at the bus stop with me, look up to the sky
Providence, Rhode Island, where RISI is floats away.
Sometimes we dream of another island:
While the worst atomic crisis since Chernobyl smolders in North Japan,
People go out for the first time with short sleeves on
The sun has taken down the plans of the building
Come to a standstill
Like a hay maker resting
Taking a deep breath in.
Bumblebees stumble
Faces shine through bankers and branches, upon roofs of Breath Knit County circling between river and pale church forecourt
There is a changeable spirit of immobility.
Over here, I stagger thinking back to my short time before paralysis
Moss-filled barns, spaces between grave markers, filling with firelight of sun
As the dancer does with pride, leaning her head down between her knees to catch an extra jolt of oxygen: hands folded into apron, because there is contentment:
    The work is done.

If Breath Didn't Knit This World

What did? Kathryn, you fold your tall form around a chair, rough merlot on hand Sibelius on the phonograph, cancer behind. Red weather of rough sailors.
Why this coat I am wearing which shimmers in the wind?
Peggle Knights, a game you play. Are they nights in armor, shining or lullabies, darling?
And why keep keeping all those little loto tickets
If you're never going to check whether you can cash them in?
What if I decide to no longer dwell among you?
A small boy named Leopold
Came down one morning from his bed chamber
And wept biter
So that the bright ears ran over his cheeks.
This comes from the *School Reader, Second Book*, 1849 New York published by Dayton and Saxon.
When I see the blue slide from your marble beautiful eyes
I know only the crust of light is disturbed
In which it was embedded:
It will shine again with all its natural splendor.
End never. Where I take my life onward from here is any place but fear:
Take for example my blue-lidded blushing bride, the pride I cannot hide:
Three wild graces and curls beside.

Lynn Strongin

I see where you ran, looking back at your heart, over your shoulder
Like a racing Irish hound
Outline pierce to the wind. I sit on a chair shaped like an H: for Hell. For Hound. Then add wheels for O and get rolling. Ovation Orpheum
Stuff of your Dreams, work of perforations:
Grommets, threads, window spins win.
Revelatory, Krystina: Salton wave, a single wave which takes off and keeps going and going:
Boomerang, the magpie, collecting its of thread with a life of their own,
A history: I wound round the wasp waist of the young ire,
I was the last silver hair pulled thru the grandmother's cap
When she wore baldness like a skullcap
When Morphine was her lover
She held the cat in her arms against the pain Morpheus; a fine craftsman commonplace law like the river passed her by.
The girls lined on either side of the classroom
Those Spelling Bees of Breath-Knit Country
Ran the world
Looking like a potato from above: from outer space breath knit world
Knit one, purl one, step forward requiring the full public in their mirror gaze to return your love, your passion
Move out there, girl.

Legs like pipe cleaners
She danced her way thru youth, scrubbed down too s with elbow grease
Why is the second way of polio so crude?
A raven dead draped over flowering rock.
Why did you come to me, blood of the swan not on your hands but in your heart?
Who had done you wrong?
I sit with little bulbs of garlic like lamps, into the genre of abstraction
Sitting in hospital lobbies
Filmic, glassed-in boxes, fire foxes
Square of fire
Waiting for my taxi ride home.
 How can that not be inscribed in memory?
Because you are already framed does not mean I have you.
Interrupting the normal flow of posts,
I ask you if this love letter posted to the door is not one too many
We could drive along the old roads to see the lambs
Downtown to wander along the Inner Harbor
Cattle Pont a walk along the sea
O Cotswolds O Cook Street
Nobody would post a cruel notice of death on one of the April posterns
Moving forward in the shadow, like two lungs breathing, of our pain
Nobody would kill the swan.

My Childhood was my Comfort

I ran backward for a handful of soft gray and ash rose petals from that brief time I can remember walking as others do.
Now I see chain holding fairytale braid in cauldron.
Turn me back from this scene, Lord
Of all living things
Enlarge my holdings:
Spelling bees, folkdances, cut out of velvet and satin, velveteen
Trumpets blowing
Blaring the light
Of hospital which with the same lungs, now hauled in two boxcars of hellish has and containing
Coals that burned the eyeballs to look at
Writing like a blind woman but will calligraphy learned hundreds of years ago, a scribe:
Each letter formed in jet ink
Standing on tendrils of toes high to reach
My handsome Anne.
If I were a boy, when I went hunting I would keep out of the way of the gun
Not to get shot
Shouldering my musket:
Now civil war fields unroll, quilted satin, before my eyes these nights, unscrolled:
It is an issue of unhappiness.
She brought her blue the color of Mary mother of God's feather duster, handed me a photograph of her family:
I asked for one.
"For my sister," later she said and I think wanted it back, all those handsome dark golden skinned ones. Bicycles I drum, take another dram, and dream:
Lord, unlock the two wings of my childhood again
Slashed balsam hugs the chains
I hear masts ringing: I bring home an armload, like flowers of the bride,
But payload today of trapped, still murmuring like hearts, stings.

Now on the edge of sleep
Things tremble
Glass babies stop at the edge of the table.
The tickets at the foot of dolls tell.
Like a tin blade, the starfish will wait.
Do canvases come circular?
Does the start of a malignancy change a personality imperceptibly yet perceived like the warm that changes to hot
and burns.
One drops a snowflake
Snow blinding
Words slip from purple's lips.

BETHANY

Go your way no the village over against you
as soon aye be entered into ye shall find a colt tied –Gospel of St Mark 11

Bethany, I will take you gently by both shoulders:
Soldier, listen to me
I want that painting desperately
It is swirls of cirrus clouds
It is the colt brought to Jesus it is over and against the enemy the tsunami
It is cut branches of rainbows off trees, sawed for Christ to sit upon
It is me flying out of the body
Crying Hosanna
What country is not lit of breath
Of lung? We are not children of a vanished world, Roman, women have run homes from iron lungs.
After you were a nurse, you studied law, now thrown from the horse, Age, you will become a navigator:
Navigate thorns of stars, stars of thorn children re-appearing
After a century's vanishing:
What county?
Blessed be the breath taking that coming
It's the name of the childly ghost.
More than a hundred ships from the Japanese 7 U.S. Militia are searching for bodies swept out to sea.

What does a cork tree know

The deer's footprint
Is left in the wet.
Yet, blown away   characteristically
Breathers and bearers in heart-knit county
be
In a hall of thousands of mirrors
and one unicorn
a fire burns:
    Ferdinand the bull is under his cork tree.
Flowering magnificently.
Flowing as he whom I love flows away:
Attendees, attendants, April Fool's day know the villain in the hero, vice versa
    Upping stakes in short fiction
    O Alabama.

Lynn Strongin

MEDIEVALLY WINTER

Red Socks

A lamp am I to thee that beholdest me.
   Amen.
A mirror am I to thee that perceivest me,
   Amen.
A door am I to thee that knockest at me,
   Amen.
A way am I to thee a wayfarer — Act of John 95
The Apocryphal New Testament trans. MR James

December 2911 (new experimental poems)

Detectable as blue birds against a white wall against a memory board that contains the only record of Bette Davis moshing. It's about Steve and Hector or impressions of them stumbling through storm weather. But it's really not about them, or their teddy bears. It's about our personal interior landscapes that fracture and wind around each other like a tornado winds around the wind. This book is about weathermen and pink-eyed women. And thermos

.

Kristin Santa Maria
Editorial Assistant
Firewheel Editions

The feet are blue the thick socks candy-caned striped
The nurse searched for her forceps from London and made the perfect release.
She'd hold up my white knee socks and mourn, our mother who said she missed the dirty pad like a kittens?
Once I was paralyzed.
Paralysis set in like a winter's night.
No windows on then one by one like spouts on the leopard appearing Celestial measles.
Suddenly my hair is silver. It is winter. I am old. A recent tumble from bed transferring to wheelchair—which has been my only way of getting around since age twelve—left eight stitches in the one foot to which any movement at all returned.

To a tree hugger.

Mother said the part of life she missed most

Maybe I wasn't praying hard enough to God.

*
"Let me tell you something about myself. I wear a hearing id."

Next day I asked, 'Have your hearing aid in?" " "I never wear it."

The passer-by of the Downs

Has taken my red fox.
They move them these days by swings, the paralytics:
Slips on ropes or chains.
Ours was the-medieval world of hoists.

Even the doctor saw why I took what I took for pain
Narcotic tranquil?
Let no mirror break this morning in this home.
"I've found the

O Pony

I could give you a kiss; the little boy said when he finished the story.
"Zoe! This is the way to walk run. Read me another story."

May my last years be gentle like a walk with the homeless in the snow?

My latest book was about nothing holding back the night
Then spinning into the fire wheel.
It was you. Nurses. Novices. Nuns.
In your red windbreak still dotted with rain now filling with tiny bites from my teeth each time the surgeon took a stitch in my foot.
"It's only pain," she said:
I saw boxcars of a Ferris wheel what a ride
In each trip to hospital between windows
At dusk from childhood to seventy
I am sure I gloss
More translucency.

Orphan Thorns

God give back *my Dr Seuss* Red and White Sox
All the publicity for the reading is out
And my beloveds
What if I am too tired to appear?
One wing drags in the mud, the other has rips into eh feathers:
These tears are little windows thru which to see God.
I shall be walking thru a snowy night with the homeless people
Anonymous, spiritual
Just over the horizon discernible there:
No iron lugs,
No apothecary blue plans. Don't get too near me or the red fox of dagger.
O confession of a great lover:
Not all my lesbias had flowers in their hair
Not all had hair around their wens
Nor that far away dreaming for my boatgirl stare.

POSTLUDE

At cock crow in Breath Knit Lane, the weathervane will radiate, black iron
The voices may stop at last: mother and father bantering
Or at the brown dusk
You will be happy again. "If I end up in an institution that will shave me?
I don't want to look like a female Abraham Lincoln" you think.
You think depressed people do not make good company. You think of
buying boxes of diapers for a bladder infection in your seventies.
                I think of your opening Dante late at night, sipping wine,
and smiles. I think of my years at the music academy.
My Thursdays were riding an elevator up floor after floor, the trumpet
came thru the elevator on the first floor, the violins, the voice ascending at
the top.
Harmony and first thru fifth species counterpoint Miss Ulelha
Who wore the neck scarves of the 1950's tightly tied at the neck as if to
strange,
Carried her handbag by the handle in front of her as women did in those
days over half a century ago: like a handlebar.
Would I sit in a brown confessor coffee shop with you I would be enjoying
myself, listening in the moment
But listening more sharply for when Sweet Pea came, the long note of the
trumpet
Winding up, down spiral stairways, belief in the self, the power of the
voice growing, growing till wings burst thru shell of sound, feathers shone
But my lover does not want to hear the German-Jewish voice of my past in
an interview
The cock crowing.

MOTHER'S ARABIAN HORSES

                     Ripple on silk batik   catch   up   with their tails:
Breathless. Out of heart but rich dark hood:
In the name of blood,
    I spent morning reconstructing a ruined pillow, delicate as hand surgery, ball by ball of cotton
Trolling on from a narrow escape
My finger shedding a fragile light
Like veil.
An Arabian batik stork flashes temperamentally his silk tail.
    Cottonwood dust flickers over barbecues coals, bats will soon take blue-black wing.
This is nothing to the killing season
When we came.
        Living on Cook Street, down from Wellburns Grocery Family Owned and Operated for over a century (And what a century in which all those soldiers live dand died, wallpaper backdrop gunmetal gray) up from the Ocean and Oxford Foods.
    Fort Street, "Antique Row" obliquely laddering up and down
        our salvation.
    I wanted to do anything to turn back, crying O native land where the brightness was culled in a basket like bird feathers
Of the mounting swan
Not the shot swan.

Is Algebra from Arabia

Orphan, you carry the whole thing
Further and further
Over the bridge
Toward forever. With dark silk lashes covering violet eyes
   A color eyes were never meant to be. I too have taken the midnight train to Georgia
   To kiss the center of the terror: the victim, burned. I have folded back the cool sheets from him, let the night wind and the June bugs glimmering in.
   Would be a genius.
   Whatever bug's in your ear, hop up and down   shake your hands like Lil doing the zambugie. It's horrifying to stand in judgment of brother and sister, so bend
   Genuflect, reflect, and smile at the reflexion, which can never be more than that: reflection.
   Childhood nightfall's and the smell of sweet hay
The smell of salty circles of urine.
   A bee in your bonnet over the maid of Orleans, Joan AND
You've got a thing on Florence because it is the real thing
like the oncologist's dictum, carries truth true truth.
   Over the bridge, tired feet but strong Italian shoe leather, you fare
Worn for the wear, worse and worse, or better and better
But capable of extras you climb the ladder.
   You are not an orphan star alone: you are tucked in with other orphan stars that reach out hands, make the saving connections like a PBX operator
   Where the stars are keypunched
   You save the whole: the glass containing marbles the color of stars. You make the long night flight to Europe Earhart made
   Savior: Our savior, the one who has kissed the floors of the asylum, known the salt of its air. I feel your struggle as a hospitalized child but I too carried the whole bloody thing further and further I respect you to bloody hell to Jesus: we know the whole range:
   Angel, Anne, Ange: it is Michelangelo tapping at your midnight window with blueprints of the Sistine.

   Feather-by-feather Every Spent Fuel Rod
   Three sheets to the wind
      Into window-weather, elbows locked we fly sister.
   Zoom.

Strip mining
Shedding tears where it gets you between the eyes:
Kite-flying with the words written on the rose-colored wind "I love you to the ends
Of the earth"
Where does earth end and we step off, take the hand of Charlie Haydn and Keith Jarret, Lucky Link.
I would not think of writing my name in water
Nor carving it in glass   I don't know how, might get cut.
This kid doesn't want to be left alone on the playing field of life
You once said when I told you I was failing.
Now I am not.
Urine circles form haloes in memories of the war.
A child sprouting cellophane wings the kind you wrap one dozen American beauty roses in to send to your dream lover at fourteen.
Stand firm in my collecting
I am drawing the curtain.
    I am drawing a picture of the curtain
Thru it angels are flying
They have skinny-scabbed elbows
They are ageless, are a trilogy, are eight or nine, and now I am thrilled to seen an even wider wingspan
Infatuation "This is how I make potato latkes."
Lean forward on your toes, whispering as a tall child does into the ear of an even taller adult:
The luminous of every ordinary thing, every geometric drawing, every spent fuel rod, every algebraic equation
and the absolutely transcendent radiance of, above all, within and outside the tradition of lace,
the whirl of one snowflake of lace made in Ghent one war time morning when all seemed lost except the fairy tale aura of creation
of war fought like trains beginning again   the overnight underground run.
The will get there, wheels oiled but will never arrive. You know the rest by heart my one and only one.

Lynn Strongin

The Moon in its Pearl & Cradle Skin

Does not understand what it shines upon.
Reading Abraham Lincoln, I close my eyes: in age.
You have gone for trans for me, for narks, let's stop at diapers.
But the water washes the stone.   God had a cradle too
Maybe. It could happen
That infancy
With laces tucked under its chins
Turned to age with bandages about the ribs to ease them
In their terminal breathing.
Abalone: Mother-of peal r: did God have a mother?
As a boy did he make urine stains?
Or leave it all to ancient crop circles
Druidical stones?
Staples hold together my manuscript, as I cross another Rubicon,
Blind, blinded, floating
Rain maker come
Stir the waters in a bowl with a wooden spoon
Silently
The liquid slaps the shape like a cone:
Above floats a funeral of grievers who really loved him, arm locked-in-arm.

Have lost my faith

Look everywhere:
No cold star,
No stone unturned.
Then I come face-to face with the rainmaker: his face partially broken:
some vessels bloom into oceans of another planet, kinder than this brute blue one
The Promised Land.
A net of blood vessels holds like the string holding the ancient Portuguese fisherman's supply of vinegar and wine.

It's not worth wrecking your heart over it, cradle-bone
Sitting, lighting up a reefer by some abandoned gas station in the desert
Above
Fireweed floats down
Drops seed
Breaks bone.
Don't lose any sleep over it, sugar, but 'd rather trade off continence for pain
That makes a mess of one's work:
Even Shakespeare's birds would shriek like harpies
Instead of David playing on his harp
Melting a heart of stone.

The water's right cold now, God
Bright was worried about me then she up and died.
This is no bed of roses, no Martha's Vineyard
Doctor shopping at midnight, barefoot to make little sound
Under a moon whose skin is cradle-skin
Rocking.
Knocking for oxycontin.
Contin means continuous the doctor told me. Learn the Latin names.
Was he putting his boxing gloves off then? Didn't he know he only drew them down from the shelf to hand me?
He was fighting someone his own size
Thought a small woman in skinny jeans and root beer colored eyes.
The water's cold outside tonight.
I've gone from vineyard to vineyard
Tasted all the wines.
For me, lock them all away.
The pain's a bone-breaker

Lynn Strongin

The air is cold outside
I was a tree leaper
A hill climber:
Shopping around, I grimace, they're rocked in cradles but knew no human birth:
They're like the blues at a Quaker funeral: so light the fire starter:
Weep, weeper. Keep a keeper
They're kept hidden
In spaces above the ten year old child's reach
They're hard on the system
They're suckers, they're bleeders:
They're stashed and stored in box cabinets like precious wines
But sure as the Lord made little green apples
and Mary was a crier: they're stamped with letters and numbers, they go down smooth but it's a rough ride: and, Lord,
But none's a keeper. Not One.

In the Previous Life

I ran a day care.
I had a little girl: nut-brown hair, darker in autumn than summer when sun bleached its rims like the touch of love, hazel eyes.
I surmise the unbelievable happened:
She could not be saved. I could not save my child:
She heard voices, they drove her wild.
She heard Italian but she had run out of me run out of space:
Would the dog sit on her nose?
Or leave her in repose, to unfurl silently the only language love knows
The tongue of the rose?
When you were an orphan, star, you had no mamma, no pp:
Now you are harboring, nestling, nesting in:
In age as in infancy, did you know a thing of pain before you were born?
Will you know a thin after you are gone?
It's only the unquellable and supreme
In between.

II.
I have never seen you in your white coat, sir, but in my life beyond I might
Knot and dry to maintain the crash look.
In their bee boxes, bees, droves, worker and the one queen who must die at impregnation, the colony before collapse, hum.
I un-love winter, can embrace autumn, but summer is my honeyed crown.
The bees in their bee boxes the color of honey win
The day: I read my beloved Dante, I shall never understand my parenting
But I place the crown upon full spine-melting summer-heat.
For me, it is light   is the distillation of all that is sweet.
I'm going to beat the pants off you, I'm going to skin you alive, voices
Which will not let me live.
I skim you like a knife paring a cocoanut in one clean, corkscrew-curl:
Of the unbeautiful, the cruel.
       Now life, go on and on forever like the unreeled fishing line in an eternal summer pool.
Sexual happiness is like watching a Roman fountain.
I only dance when all my bones are in
Place, all my convent-like holy lights on. I wear no veil, I bear a cross,

but wear no gown: When I see mother my voice box breaks, my cords snap, the sound is inhuman, that hoarse. I close my eyes to the sound of them heart of stone, how can they rob me so?

I am robed in human blood and bone. Umbilical cord blood, the best, the blest. If I gave someone a blood transfusion she would live forever maybe.

My voice is the black box of the plane: forever containing the history, with indexes, if found.

My parents they went for the jugular vein, that is my dilemma, God.

II.
I want a sugared muffin and a coke. My coke-bottle –green eyes are not like the Holbein girl I love. Those furiously wrought features, those sleeves

God paralyzed her legs. What would he who has everything want with a twelve year old's legs? He was jealous. Envy capsized him.

Give them back God! But now they're good as dead wood.

Well pull out one of my memory bank's vaults and put it on default: make them self-destruct all vivid and limpid scenes, set my hips swaying, no long arthritic

But like those of a woman in love

Swaying, coming as she's dancing.

Remarkable as Friday Kahlo's eyebrows e=which knit. She cut them from time to time but they always knit together again.

If I don't shave I look like a female Abraham Lincoln.

This bearded lady is psychotic, as twelve too many personalities, and she is bi.

She is I. I know now the face in the mirror but if I dared lean close, could I (without cutting myself?) kiss her?

Anne (I whisper to myself) Anne:

All springbok in Africa wake and wove like water, no organum, and orgasm at my name.

Over new turf I walked on feet to which the earth felt good, God.

I raised my arms feeling my spine click, unlock, freed my ribs, and drew in my abs: breathed out the fear, breathed in the love

In a great in cloud. Hunters are identified by their high boots. Lyn, you wear ink-blue "crash" sleeves, long, imprinted with paisley flowers.

As far from Victoriana as the kiss of death from that which ignites birth.

No pink elephant was sitting on my nose. My pudding bowl haircut of an adolescent Saint Joan made me smile, chainmail shed for the while.

III. (For Lynn from me, Anne)
Paralyze paralysis! Devocalize the arias
That vocalize the thievery of bliss.

Lynn, you were taught to throw your half-paralyzed body on the gym mat flinging a crutch, twirled out from either arm, balletomane, gymnast, a sprinter with words:

Angel athlete in the letter a shape of a hip roof but not safe like a house.

Like the cheerleader's batons. Only these were your sole, soul support.
Raised by the rule of light
We ledger-tread darkness too.

With the most feminine gesture in the world, our mother could removing her eyeglasses sensual, lighting a cigarette an invitation

Packing it down.

We were the generation of children taught to thrown ourselves at the floor

Like so much scattering or face, of seed,
Confetti after a wedding
Boletus
Of children:

Legs thrown first, not keepers, tossed slats of wood

In order for you to catch your body weight, all eighty-five pounds, and land on the palms. Squint eyes with the pain, shadow-soldiers from the civil war once lined these very halls.

Falling forward take care that the forearm not snap in two
and if it does you end up casted, cast in the only role meant for you: hearts and lilies and Maddie loves Jean painted all up and down.

That was falling forward.

Fling backward was the stay in Hell:

It could mean further paralysis: upon analysis x-rays would indicate that the cervical vertebrae were broken.

No more summer laps in ice pond, no more skinny dipping. It had been taken away forever as was but this was double-whammy doom.

DO anything to save yourself from a skull-soldiers still rode the underground railway midnights, taking a lady on their lap for the quick grab

Lighting up.

As for you, you were virgin, a dozen years of living packed in your skull, thighs, forearms, backbone:

Skull-cracking came fall backward: beyond the exercise mat with its mattress buttons was hardwood floor built there in the war. Fall backward: columns upon columns, Greek Ionian, Corinthian, Doric in their fluted flame like girls in first pre-adolescent nightgowns, trailers, identified how high the moon.

Ferociously, desperately try to tilt the body to some side, find a new angle

Like a needle in the haystack.

You use all you have, Lynn. You won't take no for an answer.

But that was your previous life.

Tomorrow is another geographer with compass and protractor applying for a refuge for the day.

Flash! Fling!   Dying of thirst a mild from ocean.

Rolling Wood

Keep believing in me
Slow it down, hun bun, try to slow I down I doesn't work.
Nowhere to go buy B'way and Forty-second Street
Where the violin makers worked by day
Rosined and restrung with fresh horsehair
The dyers, the plucking.
    Who ever said it would be easy? Perfume burns the air.
Anyway you turn, it's going to hurt.
Fling soldier, hit the dirt.
Lost your heart.
Blue alert.
Shopping at prince prairie, save me a song I cry. I'll try.
All you want to do it get their firs: blue hurt.
Listen, before you're a girl scout you have to wear a beanie be a baby.
Blue Alert. Hit the dirt.

How Long is the Shelf Life

Of the dream of walking?
The stilts gathered dust. Bubbles formed upon the mercury stick in the Hubbard tank:

It began at cool and was stuck forever at scalding. Let everlasting night in.

SHALL WE EVER MARRY?

Shall we do the cell phone thing again?
Answer on the third ring? Turn it of except for one hour between daybreak and dawn
Preceding the light up of the horizon but following the elegy of sleep sung by the night table in the garden. The sprit is spent by the time the curtains part like lips in song.

Turf me up at dawn
Skip the title. You say your spirits are in the gutter. My loves are too.
Scroll down:
The page is pearl   the ink the pink on the inside of the shell: the world is your oyster,
Your soul's an orphan snail. Soon to be adopted by the world.
Wastrel, do not waste me: pass me the next ball
Underhand, over land
    The faith in ramparts of seawalls is shattered
If buildings or anything here had been checked. . .there's nothing.
This village has not been reached and I have to tell you there is a fairly strong smell of decay.
    The oval portraits are coated with dust.
    But spring will shake their coats, or blow them open: they are images of a lost way: they will no stay that way.

Get your mind out of the gutter
and go up straight.
How? Thru Plato. Thru Sappho. Thru Dante
Ascend to the holy light.
Have pain pills made me incontinent? That sound d is pure comfort, is rain is Japan
Restored to Japan.
So pile the woolens, bundle them like a babe and take to the washroom.
I have drawn forth this specific photograph of an old shack in Castroville, the Artichoke heart of America:
Its whites are half a century old, its creams bleed
and in the screen gridding which lets flies in
there are arteries.
Nails stud the hip roof and there are veins
In the vertical to heaven planks of wood

So take your mind with you hold it like a helium balloon, a kite
Then when your hand cramps, let it go, amazing it will bloom
The first star quivering, quavering, a mute stuttering trying to speak
A deaf person trying with all the obedience in the world and discipline to hear:
There it will become, if you look at it long enough, Venus, intractable, invisible flame.

Lamp, Mirror, Door, Wayfarer

Ambulance ride on December Night
Nurse Jean tailing us in her car with my wheelchair.
I had not looked for it   but snow
To heal and tallow the candle.
A lamp I must become
On a mission.
    A mirror:
If you imagine all my childhood scenes flashing before me
There is the nurse in cupcake hat, or nunlike wimple.
There is the small brass bell like the librarians bell
There is a door — although I cannot push the window open
And if I could what would I see?
I can no longer walk:
    I turn green jeans, my old bleached ones
Into legs the color of grasshopper. I make a face. She giggles who is my cubicle mate of five
But for me at twelve
Above all, I am an Ishmael, a wanderer
A faith seer
Kneeling in a vacant lot, biting the dirt
Then feeling wings scratch and itch at my back
and Turning in an anger: Snow. Winter. I signed, sealed and delivered
to bite off the wrist bands and re-enter the surreal
home and live I habit.
    Of this I am sure: it is the color Peter Breughel the Elder used in his
"Skaters in Winter."
    Beyond color, it is a bell, a harp a touch tenderness that perhaps cannot teal
But just fill your eye from dot in center to outer rim of wheel
With teal. With teal.

Jan 1, 2012

Lynn Strongin

Slowly healing war's deep wounds

The light comes into the sky
Tying its apron.   A trim bow of white, lock hands behind back:
How (thinks the woman) shall I carry on?
How did I always
Then arms akimbo:
Hope stories like greased lightning   forked lightning:
She shields her eyes with her right hand, a hood an Amelia Earhart:
She is 67, has been a lawyer and a nurse:
Texts emerge as embers

THE SMALL DISH FROM GREAT AUNT JANE

    Circular
    Circularly holding our small beaded key chain
    The stuff of our dreams and desires locked in.
    I wear a dress of dust.
    Since it is winter, should have the neck ring on
    But no ring-necked pheasant, I bow, reverent, in prayer, in the stony pews of air,
    The ebony bench has
    And drink my cupful of shadows, then am done. *Amen.*

Lynn Strongin

OVERSHOOTING THE MARK

Red Feather Duster

As she fell into sleep
She could feel and see herself overshooting the saddle
Knowing sick sick feeling she was going to fall.

The nurse who went back to the forceps from London
To take out my final stitch.
She was simply trying to mount the horse when this happened:

The stirrups were too short
Getting the necessary leverage to raise her r leg up over the saddle.
Stirrups too short.

While in Asia, women are hunkering in dust dresses
Over their bowls of shadows
Stirring them.

Fall up from sleep
Rise like the bladed wheat:
Midfall, a hand that is thin but not skimpy trembling: like those eyes, now hazel
Now filled with (Renaissance woman) inspiration:
Nursing. Law.
    But truly, my lord, I it not navigation after all, how we take the bends and rounds?
    Is it not the Magi   that our faults not blanket us from transparent to opaque?
    Many as ink, and as tall as raspberry cane

Listen to W. B Yeats: in The Magi now as at all times I can see in the mind's eye, In their stiff, painted clothes, the pale unsatisfied ones Appear and disappear in the blue depth of the sky With all their ancient faces like rain-beaten stones, And all their helms of silver hovering side by side, And all their eyes still fixed, hoping to find once more, Being by Calvary's turbulence unsatisfied, The uncontrollable mystery on the bestial floor.
    Ride form sleep
    Those silver pools on the floor are handcuffs.   You want to be the best, one of
    Entering winter
    Red feather duster in hand, classically healed and well.

A white bone tray   violet flowers on it in a glass
It is my first time in sickroom. I am twelve. This too will pass.
This too, red fox, tipped with desire.
It was only because the unbleached road lead to the soul, which was unfettered, that led to this wild rampage.
This white geometry of this rampage return
Hen sunk like little crosses, abacuses:
There's nothing like the corpses of children.

What do boys learning grille wear? Gaunt of leather the color of blood.
)How is your blood tree today? Blood tree with one black apples?)

I didn't' want to wear the neck brace because Dr Zhivago daughter did and we were in New York beside, thought I was Russian.
Long leg metal braces and crutches were more of this world, the poster, and the iron. But the fur muff I associated with ice-skating became tragic ikon to me
If it eased the pain it created one great one.
Its Biblical Overtone. *One Greater One.*
There was no pain in legs a brace (hidden) didn't correct, and knee braces whose locks cut fabrics.
But the collar: it was too close to Angel. Too much that I might go to God that night. Too immortal
Ad in the dark I tried to become immortal
With the feeling.
The neck brace was soft as a bunny, however, and I took it from its hiding place in my bedside tin table with private drawer, top drawer.
We had a passion for privacy that had none.

Lofted. Elated. You who call many things not like the musk ox, extinct.
I relate, you see, I did come thru Nuremberg's town gate in snowstorm but wore vest embroidered with wool red roses because of where I came from
And chain mail, a suite of plate light enough for a small man and I was but a boy.
A girl in a Dutch mirror, silk scarf blown out, then in: sucked in. What can I tell you? It feels like nothing I have ever known. But there is still morning press, evening press and "Pa's Chair" painted on mother find, a Quaker harpack one picked up at a barn.
She was going on nine out of ten thousand syllabus. This was the nest the new kid on the bock, the apple valley revises, lives of eh artists.

You think you have it all. Whoa! Draw in those reins.
"This is the book" Remy said to the child to whom he handed the ash blue *cahier*. It was not what the boy wanted the full tree
to blow him way
desire blows him an August nightfall.
   Now orange is beautiful
For the first and only time.
You were never, at isolated moments, so happy as when we were trying to decide what to do about me:
"The Meany Towers Hotel" Southside, overlong ten anxiety clinic:
this was anxiety in incubus. when staying at "The Meany Towers hotels" adjacent to Center for Anxiety and Depression.
Here were the robber baron. Here, those bent like hairpins. Those with hatpins stuck into their head, they self-injured so hard.
I, the lark, had waked among them, to strange folded piece

One beach on one side of me, on the other., the Holy Braille I cannot write I dream.
Grab the spade black shovel,
What burns in the grate last of all is a coal red rose, your heart: the Braille read third fine boned had,
Now knot the knot of raspberry tie the boy slide under the covers and watch the rose bloom from in the fire.
I cannot go back there the four roan horses hauled the leather-bound child
But Icarian?
The north sky is the most amazing color: that early pluck string elation returns
Ovations
Orisons. Johane. Jehane. Tawny Jane.
Are you going on stage, sister Ishmael? AN I, are we both? Now that he who loved my work has died will there be others?
O early beloved altos, sopranos
The head in the socket of cast was the earl lifted gently by the nurses
Lest they glimpse the kingdom:
   Turning the hydrocephalic side's head every two hours a forty-year lifetime. She lived in a tilted green wooden box, a go-cart on special wheels: Michelle's deal.
The Broken man was coming.
I told the jacket of blood, red autumn leaves. Something or other is always catching my heart.
I told the woman with the butter suedes and voice to match: a choir of kindness

But what I told her was not the outcome:
It was the prayerful, one of god's children, even hour when like now at seventy-three I burn every mock candle
Pure wax in the house. Recall my furious days in glaze beret smoking,
My Roman Catholic friend, ex-un help by both talons lifted above the city does the same.
Juggernaut me. Get not to eh bottom of our fondest
Go out, eye reflecting globe, like the silver outside the pawnshop; into that marble curved morning
Carved in its dust the passion of Juliette's age, 14, the growing old in the mulberry home woven hymn-on-hymn, like Casa Maria for Ancient Ladies in the desert down south here.
.

It sounds like a milk and rain party.
I do not exclude the leather wearing ones,
These in burgundy jerkins
Knitting things: I will knit these two women like braid together, the chiaroscuro emotion of not too bad: Flo and Ann, Patience and Sarah
And the axe will be boot-back noise, and the autumn maple red as your blood.
Who would be so cruel not the dark as to frame her ex girl friend?

We want to rear-cut that back door,
To make a Dutch door of it
Let in the pencil boxes of morning, the bloom the boy's throat
The delicate Yoga strength of wings.
Expensive moral reform
    At overtime.
I keep looking to the South
But no sunrise
Over blackened buildings.

Creams, cool colors of vellum:
Palest dawns, lemon
Yellow gauze
All for disease that can't be eradicated: so take it just the sensitive delicate way of the ballerina doing another dance.
Look, we are doing a death dance. Not bogus. This s not Halloween
We are truly looking at girlhood still: pencil boxes stacking up in the darkened light o New York Decembers:
Though rage break bone, bend bellow tones from the sax
My prayer is to be mellow in the twilight of my life, many hues of kindness, silver braids or none, still.
In this window of my life I want all door open.

Pilgrim how do you touch yourself then come?

We all want to come. To rise up from the pews in Basque blue dancing. Not to be wallflowers with horn rimmed glasses, not to be desired.

There were two fires burning. The lesser flamer loved the larger: when the two got together, Hopkins creation bloomed:

All sorts of birds and Halleluiah stallions.

Austere porcelain :oriented with for-get-me-nots and wallpapers. That was me at twelve.

The boys lips were split, as if to blow a grass slip, a blade

The eyes the color I pictured Appalachia before I'd seen the Boue Mountain

Locked in no prison. But O the battlefield: The Merino wool

Clotted, its roses, with blood thicker than porridge too long in the pot.

    I find the end of a thread and race it, taking ferryboats in northern light, night and I have come all the way to Iceland.

To find what? These colors woven?

    Storm was coming. What came upon us all: an ironing board light?

The morning was lemon. Noon Quaker white to bone. But evening, having learned, consumed, gentled to the last act of sacrifice

Love is what we all yearn for: then slap the pavement with the cord rope

To iron the silence of sidewalks. A new wrinkle always appears.

Evening is the new word of sacrifice: rough-hewn as forest pine, white core as the cream of the willow.

    Nail nail. Rock the Cradle. Rings the thin bell.
    Gail. Grail. Ishmael.
        Robyn-Lark: Boy-Ishmael
        There is always time.

Novmebef20110

Orphan Thorns

As she fell into sleep
    She could feel and see herself overshooting the saddle
    Knowing such sick feeling she was going to fall.

The nurse who went back to the forceps from London
To take out my final stitch.
She was simply trying to mount the horse when this happened:

The stirrups were too short
Getting the necessary leverage to raise her r leg up over the saddle.
Stirrups too short.

While insist women are hunkering in dust dresses
Over their bowls of shadows
Stirring them. Sun-hungers, Tues and Weds are promised to be sunny

Lynn Strongin

I DO NOT WAKE, A WIDOW OF SAND

I do not take the sailor's widow's walk.
I look:
At Jean overshooting the mark.
I wake to see rain scrub our two white Buddha's
As of the past me as the red feather duster
But shaken in their white stone faces makes a cluster.

I AM THE FLASHLIGHT BESIDE YOUR BED

I am the lens inside
Crossing the Rubicon intrepid, beating the *angst*
 Back with wings, one of pewter, one white lead.
Old family coats
Oval mirrors
Rose bloom of the eyeball I see   when you come
Who do not overstay your welcome.
One wing of cobweb   one of tone
Bone lace solely resumed this wing.

Since I am the torch beside where you sleep, you dream
Lift me and will I like a strong gust put out the fearsome.
Life me, whatever the cost, lady, lift me
Out of here
Horseback mounting itch too short stirrups
Perhaps God held you up
From a more precious mount
A leg over the horse
Far worse than what
Transpired
     For firmer but scoured out the corers
(cobwebs, old love, oval mirrors and Quaker chairs in tact)
of even then.

Lynn Strongin

    My helper got the last feather duster, a thing of the past
    Like us, I smiled, dust bunnies blowing like angel hair   here,
there.
    Something must change or be changed.
    Who knows the damage that has been done my spine
    Light climbs the steeple tower up and down
    Who soever therefore shall break one of these least commandments
    Makes e child of a vanished world, returning like sun after rain.
    Open again to doublespread claybased books of chldhood:
    Still earth. Still waters run deep
    Channeling a life.
    The small rain down can rain.

Why is so little taught concerning Icelanders?

Iceland is a numinous island
forgiveness can always go further
touching the torture of Jesuit prayer

weaving a tale how language
relieves suffering
eventually becoming the language of prayers.

The dozen new eggs, oval, clear-
ly to be broken
an immigrant Icelander,

crossing a bridge of teal waters
could not feel stranger.
whose hands are at the end of my arms?

dawn is an accelerant.
I want to be back in my apartment in Albuquerque
be thirty smoking.

So much that is unknowable
her cat is sick
she rides the dream elevator a car between star and star.

The nerve goddess:
We each go around toting our bags of feathers:
tiredness weighs heavier than age. Thru wire-rimmed readers

you smile at me
annual
autumnal. Spectacle. you are a tall drink of water   straight up, no chaser.
It's because there are so few Icelanders?
Old ladies reciting dreams, old men peering at chess pieces. Lava. Glaciers. The brightest green grass, to match jade eyes, on the planet.

Lynn Strongin

SISTER, WHEN YOU SAW ME I HAD BLOND HAIR

Now, it is white
Bright as stars on a winter night.

Am I that winter night
scooped out
holding all this brightness, water to drink from a gourd, for you.

Deftly starting the jeep to avoid ruts.

Angel eyes, charcoal guise.
Iceland is a numinous island.
Write your dreams down, pay attention.
    What holds a psyche together is frail and strong.
    Round as an angel's embrace, a bun hot from the oven, an apple in autumn.

Iceland

You are like Iceland. Is this country's sickness cabin fever? What a cabin, walls with heat-starved roses cracking vellum paper from another cenutury. More suicides occur on islands.
　　Speculating on the ratio of glaciers to...
　　Unwinding dreams like autumn scarves from around your neck

　　Roxie's sister's sanity turning on like a light bulb
eating cherry tomatoes revolving like the suns around Saturn.
　　Build your bones. Shell your peas. The road-story manic keeping us all shivering, chattering
　　　　steering Jack Bacon on track.
　　I was hurt because I took all the twisted hands gingers,
　　　　found the perfect structure for them: a glass mason jar. And you took them out, undoing my mile of track.

Lynn Strongin

Nobody Slept that Night
signs awaited us in morning. I'd offered a girl in a film in Apaloosa for some silver.
antler and sand. Child skinny 100 pounds soaking wet

echoing off frozen
walls
unanswered screams of the night before.

Had I woken the neighbors?
as my mother
said?

I woke alone, parched,
my hair suck to my forehead, my blond hair:
I was burning, seeing razor-sharp colors of glaciers. Neither grace, nor girl I knew, nor God was there.

Half a Year Later
I dropped my cigarette
picked it up from the stretcher, put it out rolling it over.

Such translations took place here
as the tricking of Freya
the morphing of life, paraphrased into another life:
    kin are hardest on kin.
    You have had an open window to fly out   a tree to climb
    now be kind to those who suffer: look in the mirror, you are their next of kin.

Lynn Strongin

The Road veered sharply
the rutted wretch of a road
and I a pale girl in an ambulance summer night about us like lava.

I cannot take away your fear
Nurse said
But we are never alone.

So life went
Watched by the sharpest, most merciful
One.

Sleep shoved away like radioactive
banks of
snow. I did not know where to go.

The source the glacier
we'll do this part fast said the doctor
and jabbed the needle in my spine. Like saying goodbye; quick , fast
    "You did not cry."
    I cried all my tears, like lion shedding mane, pony silken comb,
the night before.

Orphan Thorns

They created a special account at the twice-around Rose
for her who went hardly anywhere: not Peapod Grocery nor Bone Builders:
She could have been a Shrewsburian.
But her bones built to their height in latter childhood—Had they warped there?
were housed in muscles, which atrophied, flesh which purpled.
She had to look to keeping them calcified or she might be an amputee like that roommate of hers her mother warned.
Chest flat as a washboard, metal, brighter when running water covered it
from the shower as a sheet of flame might a hold burning, in a movie picture. Grade D.
 D for Dog: desire and delight filled her she shopped in autumn, she shopped in winter.
when she lost weight,   caught her image in the plate glass, same as last century, that old (By now, an appaloosa's skin the wheelchair)
she went over the moon   she saw herself as that much swifter.
Red hunter jacket, that was her first fall from grace, her great expense.
      Then skirt to match
then winter cover. She'd never gone to school: here was her December coat
she was bussing to Hunter uptown
rather than being taxied there. O Twice-Around. Experienced Goods. Second-Hand Rose:
      She got out, making the crutch placement, and swing of braced leg
there, that smartly, like riding side-saddle
and got herself in there.
She was knockout. It was a killer coat, said her mother.
Of course as a student she'd been so poor, they turned back cuffs to cover
soils that wouldn't bleach clear
back to the linen grandmother
had bought for her.   It took a brain surgeon's nerves.
Hers was Wyeth's "Christina's World."
She'd never known the story but felt it: Christina was contorted, on the ground

her arms thin, her legs withered
the house loomed over the moon high and unreachable. It was all tenable
because Christina too had had polio as a child, the disease that became extinct
when we turned the millennial corner.

Lynn Strongin

    One Winter Evening, putting the tea tray down
    you a tall glass of water
      straight up   no chaser.
    I am a chaser   no crier. Long sentences are lost on me when it's an affair
    of feeling.
    Only the role for town crier for the bells that crash thru our lair.
    If you want something you write, if you make it in to the Fir, could you also pick up a green pepper? I think I forgot to get one. It should be dark green in colour, and firm. They have the real pepper flavour; the pale ones taste of nothing!
    In summer   all was water
    but colorless wasting water
    in winter
    heart light did not conceal the fear but lit it up:
    the peremptory dismissal
    the way, wading out on mud when high tide takes the bay, the innocent ignorant way wild geese are
    Educated at Haberdasher's School for Girls
    early she wore real pearls
    your mother. Here are the breakthrough pain0killers.
    But you and I? Nothing hides our insecurity but more words
    pewter   they could be other:
    sunk passion stones at the clear bottom of a flash of water.
    This is what you get   for trading Appaloosa for wheels of water-silver.

To the Ward, they wheeled the library: blotches of Ireland for the Surveyor, in teal folded roses, and so forth brown shilling romances
sepia air curling like tightly folded bud
ready to drink air
at the core of the flower.
    It was always a rose.
With a poet's imagination she saw herself going backstage
how? On crutches, holding bouquet in the right crutch hand to present her Irish actress with these flowers.
    In reality, she asked the taxi to circle the block west 53rd for close to ten minus (which she could hardly afford)
to enjoy the vicarious pleasure twice:
it was intense   but became intense
These nights, she closes her eyes when the oyster catcher flies over
the longing of her marriage bed (in her penny romance) was fulfilled
fleshed out
over-the-mooned by the color oyster.
    That was another thing: she must search high and low for a blouse, it must be satin, with leg of mutton sleeves
    in of-oyster.
    Pearls would go with it   it went without saying. She went at it like gang busters:
over hill and down dale. The hill the slight Amstel-like rise of the Avenue to the village, too sharp an incline to push: (Shed dream-studied and dream-memorized the Belgian town: its architecture was carved into her breastbone.)
    The dale, that muted silken goddess, nerved, but who burned season-after-season in the Hades of unfulfilled desire: the dale, that traceable to childhood hell.

PART FOUR
APPALOOSA SILVER

Orphan Thorns

She had Blueprints incised in her sternum
footprints in an old hotel converted to apartments: it was carved up into 6: they shadowed her. One had a loft and moving ladder like libraries.
The nerve Goddess oversaw her at all times.
Plunk ye down and look here: Have a listen: we all must create occasions
carved out of a particular place and frame of mine.
I took up fragile architectural paper
and the right architectural tools, a pen the type city-planners
use, a loop, pulled out the old drawing board and magnified rooms.
Wrote prose but only quick footed prose with endurance
But still I was shadowed by Death and when you're being shadowed by someone you're under the gun.
Uncle, a draughtsman, built a drawing board, which reminded me of a drawbridge
it was lowered by a chain above the hospital bed.
Later he designed the big black ship's wheel kind, which I knelt over long
(the back brace, Iron Maiden kept me upright) beside our black velvet Steinway baby grand in brown velvet Manhattan sundowns. The drama of my music twinned the drama of the times.
So, upon the first , I hung my every note
on the second I went sailing. There was ocean in the boisterous skies by then.
Storm was opera: coloratura the lightning, contralto the big bosomed rumbling and thunder. I smiled at my second drawing board.
"Appaloosa Arias" I wrote at an angle.
Childbearing was now beyond me.
    I would have pupils in many classrooms:
    I needn't draw myself to overlook them. Not on your life
on braces and crutches before some old world lectern hauled out of the college basement   like my surrogate husband:
Common-law wasn't so honored then.
I hardly knew what Pussy was back then.
    Dapper, with a sense of public character (Melville and Hawthorne scholar)
    An Amawkinologist, he gaffed, Ph.D. from Harvard, one brown eyed Jewish boy gone
    crazy for heroism: French tie would do, but what beat it hands down was the bowtie: he was a performer, a lecturer, being viewed by the future generation.
Bowtie, but I often thought how swish the French tie would be on him. How could he win me more than he had won? although his hands, his

elegant hands, were up to the looping, folding French silk
    (failing that, Italian.)

When he was paymaster
>	at an army training station in Oregon,
enrolled because a Jew and had a conscience.
Wakened at night to put out a fire in a small pine
"Cut!' he called to the two men.
>   They cut the wrong direction
which severed his spine, killed the private at his right
>   and left side, (heartside) the private walked away untouched, flawless baby skin.
The movie was made after his life *The Men.*
It always rained in Coastal Oregon.
He hopped out his jeep, tall back then, and delivered pay.
They created a special clothing account at the Second Hand Rosie just for me.
"Special for Nan" the Chinese corner grocer promised over the phone.
Occasionally, I fell for window things:
an Irish sweater *Carraigdonn* wholly knit in Ireland of Merino wool
12 type stitches "selection of" were printed on the back of its label. When you consider I was about to go out in
>   Celtic and Honeycomb; Irish Moss and Tree of Life
and it was summertime. The anatomy of a love cannot be sawn off beneath the bellybutton.
>   Imagination builds. You know how deep the Celtic cross was incised
>   with love for my paymaster paralyzed from the waist down
>   called out, and gone, a Harvard student who would become housemaster
>   in time, a Leo who knew boys who said "Where my face was, there is fire"
>   you know how profound the pain and the carving (Aran Island the pullover comes from) had been for him. By him.

The Translator's Hut

on the side of the mountain has had a break-in
She has few earthly treasures: her cat is her treasure, her photographs of the divas.
It's not as though she were translating a best seller.
She is working on Benedictine sisters.
Like white candles lit the waxen images of them, holding candles themselves, entered her room.
I think of the stable, the mews, the riding habit, the crop.
Then stop
myself with an audible "No!" holding forth my hand as though toward traffic.
The translator gets colder and colder,
slips on a black cardigan sweater, the color of coal
she is afraid of death   to the point of horror.
She lights a votive candle beside her cat Gigliola.
Some say, dying scenes of one's whole life pass before your
eyes:
her life has been so sad that this would be the final insult
like gathering a scoop of ash
rather than words   all those down to brass tacks tea parties with psychologists,
and living in the house of cinders.
    Yet beyond, the miraculous dawn opens
    tangerine-orange
    simply like the five fingers of the hand.

The Usual Public Grumble

                is it cold in Berlin?
People, the government, the bad coffee
People hunched at tables.
Let's climb the wooden platform:
Look at the old wall before it's a last torn down.
Think Atonement. Amsterdam. Walk home along the line of your meditation.
Get real as mother said once
Woundfull.
The blast of cold air that leaves a cloud prancing like pony before the two European women going to their polio patients in old New York at is
To think that this was my life: the best mother could recruit from the overflow wards at Willard Parker.
The great polio ward was my backfired my battlefield
Strewn with bodies of children
Some flung free as those from a basket of children sleeping:
Some circled tight as kids shot thru a bungalow
Other casted
Recast
They'd play another part
The boy with dislocated hips
The girl with spinabifida
Would sing love songs back 7 forth to one another
A lord and lady
Fairytale price and princess
Come back God Lord in the wrong skin

The Narcotic comes every ten minutes
The one I am on bends a caring nurse or mother
To gaze into my eyes to cache if the brightness is still there.
It is. It hasn't been swept away like the streets of New York City
All paper boned off them
Like a Buddhist's monk shaved
Skull so bitterly pure
Bare nude
Shining at another New York City Dawn.

Orphan Stars

We are orphan stars, climbing the circular back stairway to bed
Holding our candles
Lying down. No one will tuck us in.
We do not know our birth powers
We are orphan stars, old children
Nobody tucks s in at night
The lace under our chin cream colored
The whites of our eyes rolling suspiciously behind a veil in inexhaustible tears.
    I am being pulled along, in an invisible boxcar, with a few other orphans
    In translucent thread, boxcars
    Each holding our candle pressed close to sternum that it night ignite
    Toward the minimal horizon:
    Listen, up, Foundling:
    No two snowflakes are alike.
        I am addressing a sister-physicist, a soul mate who dies o exist.
        She kissed the string teddy goodnight, the pilling wools that stood out
        Like clots of farina in oatmeal in the Brit Mist.
    I am an orphan but I am a star: six points like the cubes of the bees:
    Wheel to the foot my ward cot to find out that I am.
    I'll do so to yours to learn who you are.

Rain is the Language of God

When all else is spent. Parched, the tongue sticks to the roof of the mouth:
The words are there but cannot get out:
I don't like the look of blues about your mouth:
Looks like your train's pointed south:
Children trapped in a school fire.
Adolescences slitting themselves.
There is no other than the self.
Shutdown. Meltdown.
The language of God is coming
It is not snow
(which came at first) nor is it hail
To hold
Hold back the flood
Ugly black grasses blowing: we turn to what we read
As children: for comfort: AS for our nation, it dropped the ball on some big ones.
I hold my breath: and feel the stub
Of ear bone:
I grab a marble the color of blood.

Lynn Strongin

I AM WATCHING STARS RISE IN SKY

round the tipped bowl of evening
"A Mirror is either flat or deep" Adrienne Rich
Lips of glass
A Dog standing by the edge of a rock.
Am lonely I must say with Pride that Wilo gave me a look of sudden admiration.
Orphiana   God was absolutely free as the morning breeze in the ward
Even when we were served streaky bacon.
"You are more mystical than I thought," leant forward and said my friend.
Artesian dances in the orphanage, everyone is dancing, is I modest or arrogant to enter the scene?
All those hours alone on the ward
Collecting crystals of moments in bottles like tears in a lacrhymareum
Was I really imagining you Hugh, some aspect of your grandeur in your garment?
A hem to bed and kiss, a sleeve to pluck?
Who else could have left me so full of yearning in a cold March rain?
Every single web glazed with wear,
In ditches, along sills
Up to the level till
Who else so fragmentary ye wholly
Divested of the false
Rue, blue?

Objects of this world, 'Depression, raggy bears, Elysium
Do not, from this world, prefigure the next.
Our laces under coffees, leaving rings on wood,
Our footprint
Our sandals with pebbles carving ankle flesh
Hose and even the puddle we cross is unique.
 The look is unreckonable,
An appetite, a hook
For the wild iridescent fish .Our lungs, with portable suitcases containing now emptiness
Now choking us with richness of a Chinese screen
Elk, antelope, the gnu
True as well of the intelligence.
For Girls Raised by Nuns, for Girls Raised by Wolves
Mid-afternoon, beginning to inch in, an incisor
Pain up against morphine.

Emptiness can bellow, be opened and closed, like an indigo accordion.
Keep cough drops nearby.
In Stonehenge rock are arranged like the crystal of snowflake cut with rubber child's scissors in k thru 4.
A plan.
Simply set on top of a Peruvian bureau
To be scoured clean as a vessel
Whether porcelain, wood, or plaster;
Whether silver
Tarnishing, always vestal, bridal, a mystery involving many people
Without release, yearning for body upon body (Eden, each me, hold thrall, tendrils and all too alone
There's still time for impulse to cut into this dance, the sternest of all budgets
Rent to shreds in lent.

A Bookish Town

We live as we must live in a bookish town.
Slamming round corners in slacks and moth-eaten sweaters.
Initially, it was gin. Twister, I tell you we needed that slice of lime.
We were all of a sudden and after thirty and forty years in the Limey town.
Gin can be dangerously near still, like smoking *Sopranos, Black Russians,* brought forward with a daub of the palette knife
easily. The elegant gold paper at the tip, the rest of weed wrapped in black paper. What an elegant way to dig the box to our tomb.
Fate dropped us off, let us down in a railroad apartment: To boot, love-letters from a couple-buster back in the old time, rubber banded on the desk.
Too old to snap at red herrings.
No one I could phone. It got me where I live, the move: my voice.
Gone gone gone. weeks of time in the rainy season.
All the British pigeons had come home to roost.
They rustled feathers in our lobby. They muddied the waters by comments such as "She
has the pension. But just look at her area carpets."
"She's the highest social climber I've ever seen." We ate Raspberry fools from Marks and Sparks, she wore lisle stockings and ca[s as Islanders always do

Queen-Calm these days. Thirty years later.
Finland calls, calls. Magic, mystic under siege. Finland spreads a bed sheet
puts a lake down in our midst
we are mesmerized by teal green glacial moraine. This is our lace, our linen.
She has wit. She has great wanting tempered by wisdom.
Her hotel has an Irritation room.
      Loving Liszt
The Abby (nose warts and all, and frock
She gave grief to the soil a miniature Versailles upon becoming a widow:
This is the Doge's palace. Dalmatians bark on fire trucks of longing:
she rises in the heat, *Merde* on July. August is no better
She rises in the private language of bees
her noble, North aerie:

turning today into a Victorian afternoon, she lets shade fill the room:

her shadow drapes a born-in-the-last century woman: delicate, desiring:

she drops the needle on "Kalevala" She closes her eyes, sips wine, she has:

she puts Liszt on.

Half a Pill Slicer

One side is tenements with bathtub gin
the other Usher's Scotch and Beefeater's Gin.
One half the tub would be all you'd need to bathe an invalid in.
Consider those baths for the Hiroshima Maidens.
    Doubled over first of all by pain
for us polio kids it was contractions.
Yet it was all this girl dreamed of:
Hot (not to the point of scalding like the Hubbard tanks we were
bathed in to loosen our limbs.)
    These days, wearing Cape Seventy across my broad shoulders
(It's not for nothing the Lord gave me broad shoulders)
I take half the pill for morning pain:
Half for afternoon.
            For the buildup by evening,
It's almost curtains
But with a cup of tea, another poem,
I buy time.
My savings now spill over the coffer
Though still there is division:
            Old Glory torn raggedly in half with The Union Jack;
The boy in me given tough rules but freer rein
Than the girl
Who hardly sits home:
    the woman who no longer knocks back gin
but sees all thru a lime-like scrim.
Is it envy for those walking?
It's envy for a straight backbone:
    It is a house burning over the lip of the face now
stealing all the features. And they told me I'd be a beautiful old
woman.
    I traded
    Traded the brown dog of youth, sometimes pinto, climbing barns with
me
    as far as he could climb—for the Saint Bernard of the child sickroom.
    Patiently, The patient, she rolled her eyes every few hours. She rarely
barked
    understanding my situation.
She was invisible to all but me
standing in her Florence Nightingale White and gurney brown.
She once knocked a cradle over with her tail wagging.

Across the bridge
not so famously, my mother was born and my grandfather buried. My homing instinct is strong and moody.
We all want the wardrobe, the old days back not remade: just old as they are
feeling the tangy salt lime sea breezes through the open window above the Boardwalk where the old ladies peered out
from their tiny retirement apartments and snuck out on hot days in their borrowed finery, from the past huddled up against the heat and sat motionless on benches, or stared at passersby.
I have so many days worked over the line
my grandmother not famously from Bucharest
the other close to infamous from Odessa. Crossing over they took on the Rubicon
that free-floating anxiety followed them around: an albino palomino, a dog, and a shadow
in birthing rooms, in cabbage-cooking kitchens.
Good conversation. Lots of love to accept and give
spilling into every bee and oracle
at last the women
like the men   the girls and women Pinto or Appaloosa riding
under mottled skies, at last their sole source on the rise.

STINKS IN HERE

The blind, hydrocephalic child said from time to time.
Was he miming the nurses like when he said, "He's having a good pooh."
Did he understand his words?
There was no unanswerable question why
Children's' wheelchairs had to be scrubbed down so often especially the sling or rattan seats
With a religious passion
As though the Irish washerwoman were taking out vengeance upon God
Who brought down upon them all this unforgivable stench: "You look like death warmed over," she said one day to our Wee Geordie.
It as a dragged-thru-the-gutter look she conveyed to us.
In that slangy way we had of talking about pain and even death
"I was born with that mutinous look" she once told me, Bridey.
God and all his watchmen are looking, she'd smiled, when a child was brought in smiling after baptism.
"May the devil give you the mange to impregnate you so you bear a kitten!"
She said when Katie pooed one too many times.
No matter how she scrubbed and the ward scrubbed.
That was why the ward smelled so strongly of carbolic acid. The war of the disinfectants, the blue army of ironclad men with hideously overdeveloped biceps
Long before the ear of "Mr Clean" he was ready for a knockdown dragout
His boxing gloves were never put on the shelf.
At times, in first spring, the scent of dwarf hyacinth would float in, those circular bubbled baby grapes. Why it was and who I came from the village of Boxy Flame, dark salt
In the folds of the dirndls of women dancing, a lost romance
On the table, the cards. All the books of the avenue in my annex:
From the cemetery on the hill
Its smokes of lilac mixing with the stench from the crematorium.

Quake, where do we take off our shoes, where do our burying? Will there be room for crying? Straw is stacked high, far from the stake for a dreadful burning. Immolations. Self-immolations. To know my own blood came so close. It bares a nerve to judge. This fuel pool is spent. Miserecordia of judging.

A river is now our grave, waters carry our bodies along

Like wildflowers, debris from lossened factories, loosened unnaturally like clouds from the sky:

Drawn salt.

Biblically

Other places, thinner pattern notches, satin.

Weight on. Weight off. The door swings closed, open, door with a round window so waiters don't bump into each other.

It's hard to love a disabled person the whole married life on, the pressure increasing

Lie light rings thrown round the moon.

I catch horseshoes; I am the nail in the grass

I am a nest of Russian dolls

Leading to a place where shadows have voice.

Chinaberry fruits evoke a place to nest, or none: the Chinaberry and the boy's burnt body.

The chickens burst into white outside the orphanage: the stars have painted then, gone zany.

My e-mail a Quaker dance. After the ashes, comes the scattering

He e-mail with a Dickensian intensity

When one wishes to sing, to register on some one's spinal cord, jingle ear bones, slam

But gets only an altar with a dead god stretched

And prayers which have no grace granted,

The mind weakens: goes on stilts

That splinter

No clemency.

Tileworld of suicides

From the eleventh floor.

All my poems are because they must be. Have I not promised myself a haven somewhere? Where one doesn't have to live in fear of no longer gong thin

Thru ice?

From an orphanage,

From the steps of an asylum

Landing as a child, orphaned, can there be God, sweetness, forgiveness, greenery?

On which side of the bookend does the hard drive stand?

Pointing toward West Virginia or East?

Priests' cars lined up for mass

When you were still an altar boy. The operator has managed to restore light in the control room.

Poet envy can be poet suicide so I wall not imitate and write "The Everest of your bed linen."

But I hope the judges who placed my work in one slot or another
Feel as much self-betrayal
And doubt s I am feeling getting lost in this darkest world
Of language. It is has its victims
But behind always is the crowd of rascals
The weight of bones
The longing
The leap-frogging
The piggyback riding
The climbing trees
and leaping streams. I hope that all judges come away with the solemn sad feeling they could be wrong.

the daring drop a lit match down an abandoned railway station depot
where there might be gasoline:
not to see architecture melt
but in hold of the bald simple core:
the hope of being found No longer orphaned.

"A scourge of small cords"
So he made a whip out of cords, and drove all from the temple area, both sheep and cattle; he scattered the coins of the money changers and overturned their tables—St John.13

Boxy Flame
These homegrown Sundays where root balls tangle.

Yes, now it is in this very room or ones like it similar to Russian nesting dolls Martuyenshka dolls
That our life has evolved: will in the cocoon
Mulberry tints our lives
Multiples, triplicates:
Three-way mirrors, triptychs.

Hunched up on this bed in this sepia room, tobacco still a lure, what are we, sad little outlaws

I sit with my ancient things, their hearts beating, driving them a moment older.

Amtrak. It's secret secret but I hope she comes up my Go Bird
My Auntie Glo
Call me. I would grab a few of my wireless, laptop dresses and go

Orphan Thorns

    A long legged horse-back-riding northern girl
    I'd make a killing
    Not killing the swan or heron.
    Backlit: so you can hold comfortably in sunlight and dim
    I have done everything but write the introduction including taking ivory and Kleenex to wash the inside of the telephone.
    Now there is nowhere to go, everywhere I have been, homegrown Sunday, tangled root balls, boxy flame.

    12-year-old I shivered in July, knees ruckng up bed sheets, my Switzerland,
    in all that whiteness, I had a shawl thrown across my shoulders knit by Aunt Jane. Hunkered in bed like an Asian child with rice bowl (Show me something exotic, nurse, take me, Mother to Spain!)
    it quivered the jerry rigged board my Uncle the sailor sanded for me to write at
    it swung like a scimitar   on chain. Medieval during a polio epidemic in New York City summertime. Mid-century. Mid nothing else.
    I felt I'd be Quasimodo for life
    Will we grow old in a corner dark as this Sunday, you my beloved woman, and I?
    At age twelve I put on the cloak of imagination:
    Grew wings, Hermes delivering news:
    At fifty I watched our mother have
        Mini-blowouts of the brain, riding earth thru stages of light:
    I remember the African songs of my adolescence: Marias & Miranda.
    Just plugged out lights.
    Had a sexy voice, crossed legs with a swish a phone operator she was
    But her choices tell her so many things counter, contrary
    Countervailing peace
    Teachers wash backpacks found at their devastated elementary school by the bank of a river in Otsuchi, northeastern Japan, on Sunday. Motoki Nakashima/The Yomiuri Shimbun/
    Triggered a tsunami that barreled onshore and disabled the Fukushima plant, complicating a humanitarian disaster that has killed well over 10,000 people and left hundreds of thousands homeless.
    Two workers are being treated at a hospital for possible burns sustained from wading into the contaminated water.

    Iowa, I walk across the clear water
    The still water
    In you   quiet land, Breath knit County, Peaceful land

Where women speak in melodious low voices, intoned.
Tuned in
To disaster, heartbreak, I hear a whippoorwill and think poor Will.
Could it be just last spring I started out in my shop Ryder with full confidence
Then the battery kicked up a storm, I stalled at the library
And have never returned
To that freewheeling freedom of faith.
Help me down, Lord, the ladder is steep:
Wings heavy at my back now as wet drapery
Coming down form such a high
To old string the teddy bear
Who hugs, comforts me.
Then day
    Grows comfortless as its ally the gray roiling day
And she down the long hallway
Once and forever loving me holding me
Flower shop horseback rider house to house
Like an amputee with one foot pedal to a wheelchair less
One less part to manipulate and curve or bless
I fuss, I fiddle with the useless:
The most relevant thing about me is not the most traumatic: the fairytale narrative of having had polio:
I lift the holy tones and across Iowa, wheatless in winter, or cornfield high as an elephant's eye you need a ladder to get to in summer:
Let people envy inspiration. I have no ruse I do not use: I am used to glow as I go like snow.

Put on your finest
One morning I went out to buy a grand piano and found the Apollo Baby Grand, pre-World War II Chicago.
Now I'm in the market for a smaller one, a spinet.
Let's see what kind of deal I can haggle, swing
A ball of numbers at the dealer.
It isn't my finest hour:
    That was back when, bronzed, I climbed down trees upside down
Finery borrowed from the sky:
Tall elms, fir trees, sun moving over my body
Like the hand of the lover
Over the parts that have a feeling like no other one.

A miniature Crabtree in the bay window of the antique dealers
A merry g o round with five polished ivory horses
Bovine tusk the woman was fast to assure me.
Nodding I saw cows o old cream jugs getting me started, fated to spend the rest
Remainder of my life bayed blogs, bars
A prisoner of war. Ready to see God?
Not criminal but an honorable captivity.
Unfurl the nurse's crusht purple bag: unspoon medicine: she cuffs the sock, she cuffs the shirt: cuffs the day
Rocks to sleep the dollhouse baby.
But t's out of kilter, the nursery.
So do I assent to this one? In the other case I let myself down from a tower sixty feet high but my rope too short, I sustained a fall, disabled me so prevented escape.
Good morning, Doll of single Caution, Bishop of Beauvais, paid blood money, brought Joan to be tried for wearing male attire. I have none
To bring me to trail and mine are other impieties:
We worked it out about the baby pillow
Still the terrors kept ticking:
Letting oneself down into the dungeon of childhood (Donjon) the rape
The arrested movement began with an innocent miniature Crabtree one winter morning: ice drawing the window as though ice were sash.
A microclimate like that underneath the merry-go-round
Which became a darkness ground into the eye like crematory ash.

Orphan Thorns

Mirror memories abide / slide sideways
The house doubles, deep down
Almost at the bottom of the well
Buckling, rippling when wind stirs the river-
Water.
The Lantern Man also is throwing down his flame like dart shot to bottom of pond:
His miniature House above soil twins   with   wick   and   four glassed sides
Aquamarine.
Water bends, a backbend, hair tossed back seaweed dragging urchins
The letter-man's envelope with postage stamp the color of ruin
The bearer of bad tidings drops the envelope which
Is soaked like cardboard in childhood's painting room with a broom blurring.
Stars know they shine.
    Paid a price for athleticism of youth:
Glassine.
    Morphine
The girl with the coke bottle green eyes now bargaining with old man death
Still winning
Wax polish shines out of a darkness ash as the underside of a carousel:
Imagine a chid hiding under a merry-go-round.
Apple of my eye, frost is on chill rouge-red
skin.
Lustrous the hive we mine honey in. A memory no longer dropping in plumb line
    shatters tinsel like a bullet fracture in all directions shattering bone.

Anemone Sidecar #11

I reach out for my steadfast,
My God, I cry out your name, saviour
Whoever forgot the saying, forget the Light: Shoot the Shadows?
I capitalize when I do like Dickenson: Emily knew the truth is best told slant
Like organ heft on winter afternoons.
Pale blue chalk dust swirls in air as though the ceiling of the Sistine were hammered by hate.
   Unloved can do that
   The banister crumbles to powder
And one foot is already lowered.
Shot, tossed into a pit with all the others we flowered
Rising in roses
With purple vests cross-gartered.
Caught mid fitting the foot in stirrup:
A double lens shot. Moan or make music like a moorhen?
Let's run thru all our money then commit double suicide like Romeo and Juliet.
The sounds of the trains in the distance are uranium:
Are treasure trove like re-opened graves of the Jews in Europe.
Nurse with plum purple savior bag out at dawn, back at noon, out at dark again:
Cancer, diabetes, radiating: all stars in the constellation
Of orphaned and orphaning life. Open-eyed meditation. Closed-eyed prayer: you drink some darkness
Then a cup of light that burns the open and closed space archived from your ancestors in dark shape swimming on a winter's night
The Balalika playing. O you born in D.P camps, the great Haymarket that the gray goose carrying the firstborn daughter flew over
Red flannel on Old Mama's head, her babushka
   O abandoning God, I repeat from my speller: *timber, glass, inkwell, glass marble, ice*
Until the whole lace baby bonnet not of string but steel is woven and daybreak
Steals over the skull
Of Rome, Belgrade, Paris, Prague   as the nurse light hour dawns
The gravedigger's shift breaks off
Nonetheless see the Compassion open, the sun close and reopen

The light pouring the rookly cut, now chipped, Waterford Glass from great Aunt Jane whose portrait in the oval frame mirrors
Hers in the oval looking glass.
Look in the glass? O Lesbia, Penelope, Jane: This too will pass.

You came home to find me tying another color berry to the rowanberry tree:
Must ignite the orphaned, the stars, the embers glowing
Menacingly
Piercingly
The ceiling belonging to Michelangelo's Sistine: as in childhood, it's get up, your bed upon your back.
It's do or die.

WHO IS LYNN STRONGIN

Lynn Strongin was born in New York City in 1939 to Edward L. Strongin, a research psychologist, and Marguerite, an artist who studied with Alexander Archipenko. Strongin's younger sister, Martha Strongin Katz, was the founding violist of the Cleveland Quartet. During the war years, Strongin's father, then a psychologist working with injured and shell shocked soldiers, was posted to numerous locations around the eastern and southern states

Her family travelled through the south when most establishments prided themselves on their "no negroes, no Jews" policy, which affected her deeply and explorations of those experiences are found throughout her writings.

In the summer of 1951, Strongin contracted polio at the age of twelve. After a brief stay in a New York hospital, she was moved to the New York State Rehabilitation Center in Haverstraw in New York where she stayed in the children's ward for six months.

After graduating from high school, Strongin first studied composition with Vittorio Giannini at the Manhattan School of Music then transferred to Hunter College to study literature.

She graduated cum laude from Hunter in 1962 and, having won a Woodrow Wilson Fellowship, went to Stanford University where she earned an M.A. in 1964.

After graduating from Stanford, she taught at various post-secondary institutions in New York state and California. It was when she was teaching in the Berkeley/Oakland area that she connected with writers such as Denise Levertov, Robert Duncan, Kay Boyle, Paul Mariah, and Josephine Miles.

In 1971, she received a National Endowment of the Arts (NEA) Creative Writing grant. Her first book, "The Dwarf Cycle", was published the following year. Her studies in 1977-1978 were supported by an American Association of University Women (ASUW) Fellowship.

During her time in Albuquerque, her other six books of poetry were published. Her book, "Countrywoman/Surgeon", was a candidate for the 1979 Elliston Award.

In 1979, Strongin moved to Canada where she still resides.

Made in the USA
Charleston, SC
30 March 2012